Cyber Buis closed his eyes, reliving the time when, in communication with Central Intelligence, all had been made clear to him. A discovery stolen from a secret laboratory of the Cyclan and passed on to Dumarest. The affinity twin which could give one mind the power to enter the body of a prepared host and dominate it. A means to extend the rule and power of the Cyclan to every inhabited star.

The correct order in which the fifteen molecular units had to be assembled was the secret Dumarest carried in his brain. One which would be rediscovered given time—but possible combinations ran into millions . . . into endless years which the capture of one man could save.

Dumarest!

Buis opened his eyes and looked at his hand now closed tighter than before. Dumarest was on Juba—he was certain of it. It was only a matter of time now before he was caught.

INCIDENT ON ATH

E. C. Tubb

DAW BOOKS, INC.
DONALD A. WOLLHEIM, PUBLISHER

1301 Avenue of the Americas
New York, N. Y.   10019

Copyright ©, 1978, by E. C. Tubb

All Rights Reserved.

Cover art by David Bergen.

DEDICATION

To Pete Watts

FIRST PRINTING, JULY 1978

1 2 3 4 5 6 7 8 9

PRINTED IN U.S.A.

Chapter One

The figure was becoming far too bizarre in its depiction of pain. Thoughtfully Cornelius studied it, unsatisfied; no one locked in a personal hell of torment should present the likeness of a clown. The jaw was disproportioned and he altered it with a touch of the brush. The eyes, deeply sunken beneath flaring brows, held what could be taken for a glint of ironic amusement and the mouth, gaping, seemed to bear the ghostly vestige of a smile. Only the body gave him satisfaction; thin, gaunt, the ribs stark, the stomach a taut concavity, the musculature harshly delineated. The toes, like the fingers, were indrawn in the semblance of avian claws.

A man suspended by lashings holding his wrists to a beam. One left to die in insolation. A simple theme—what had gone wrong?

Irritably Cornelius set down his brush and examined the painting with minute care. The background, a coiling mass of amorphous vapor, was deliberately neutral as was the foreground, a raw expanse of sand and stone. The cross-beam, like those supporting it at either end, was of rough wood depicted with the same lack of fine detail in order to throw the suspended figure into greater prominence.

A man hanging, naked, lost in a universe of pain. One alone and beyond even the concept of hope. A human creature in the last stages of terminal agony. A victim. A sacrifice.

And yet, somehow, he had missed capturing the essential ingredient. To simply depict pain was not enough; there had to be an affinity between the viewer and the subject. A delicate communication which would be marred by the slightest inconsistency. Surely he had the details right?

Cornelius leaned back in his chair, thinking, blinking to sigh with vexation. No, he had not been wrong about the anatomical details. A man so suspended would have the entire weight of his body thrown in a constriction against the lungs which would require a constant effort to ensure an intake of air. Death would come by asphyxiation but before that would be the struggle to survive, muscles tensing to ease the constriction, those muscles turning into areas of screaming torment when assailed by cramps. And even when they failed to support the weight and so ease the constriction death would not come swiftly. A man could hang in such a position for days and, if provided with a block on which to support his weight, even longer.

A thought, and for a moment he considered it, then shook his head. To add a block, while enhancing the symbolism, would ruin the composition. A second cross-beam would have to be added lower down and would provide a distraction to the eye. An upright surmounted by a cross-piece would serve, but that would eliminate the frame in which the suspended man was centered. No—man was trapped in a prison and the beams were symbols of that. A cage grounded in dirt in which he could find nothing but death and pain. A limited universe which held only anguish.

But how to convey the message?

How to eliminate the distracting hints of amusement in eyes and mouth? The touch of the bizarre? The glint and twist, the subtle but damning suggestion that everything was a joke and death itself the final comedy?

"Cornelius!" The voice came from beyond the arched doorway causing little tinklings to murmur from the crystal chimes hanging beside the portal. Ursula, of course. Who else could create music from shaped and suspended fragments of glass? "Cornelius?"

She entered heralded by the whispering chimes, tall, slim, graceful as she crossed the tessellated floor to stand beside his chair. She was all in blue, a variety of shades which included her eyes, her lips, the sheen of her hair. Deep colors rising from the sandals which hugged her feet, to her cinctured waist, the swell of high and prominent breasts, paling as they rose to frame her softly rounded shoulders with azure, deepening again at her lips, her brows, the crested mane of jewel-set tresses.

"Cornelius." Her hand fell to rest on his shoulder, long fingers tipped with richly blue nails, tinted skin a background to the gleam of gems set in wide bands of silver. Looking at the painting she said, "Another composition. It's superb!"

"No."

"You are too critical. That man—I can feel his pain."

"And?" He shrugged as she frowned. "Is that all you see? A man in pain—nothing else?"

Her hesitation was answer enough. He had failed and by working on now he would only accentuate the failure. Later, when less tired, he would again examine the painting.

Rising, he applied solvent to his hands, ridding them of traces of pigments. As he worked he said, casually, "Did you enjoy your swim?"

"It was exercise."

"And Achiab? Was he also exercise?"

"When you are hungry, Cornelius, you eat." She turned to look at an unfinished statuette. "You were busy and I was restless. Achiab was a means of passing the time. We enjoyed an interlude, together, though, I must admit, I was disappointed. He was not as I remembered."

"Perhaps he, too, was merely hungry?"

"Perhaps."

"Or," he said dryly, "maybe he was simply bored."

She turned, stung, meeting his eyes as he finished cleaning his hands, her own eyes hard beneath the finely drawn arch of her brows. For a long moment she stared at him and then, shrugging, turned away. A whisper came from the chimes as she headed toward the door.

"Ursula—I'm sorry!"

She paused and turned, the suspended chimes catching the vibrations of her voice, providing a muted accompaniment to her accusation.

"You checked—why?"

"An accident."

"What I do, where I go, whom I see—what are they to you?"

"It was an accident, Ursula, you must believe me." He gestured toward the painting. "I was studying this. The figure seemed wrong and I was checking anatomical detail. And then, I suppose—"

"You checked." Her voice cut short his words, caused tinkles to stream like liquid notes from the chimes. "You asked and pried. You had to know where I was and what I was doing. Why?" And then, before he could answer, she added, softly, "Is it because you are in love with me, Cornelius? Is that it?"

A way out and to accept it would be to save his dignity. And there could be truth in it—why else had he wanted to know where she had been and with whom she had spent her time? A subconscious urge? An association of ideas? He glanced at the painting—no, that was ridiculous. And yet love could be considered to be a prison and the victim of the sweet madness as firmly trapped as any prisoner.

The sweet madness—why had he called it that?

"Cornelius!" She had moved to close the gap between them and now stood so close that her perfume was thick in his nostrils. A heavy, slightly acrid scent, but one which went well with the full sensuality of her lips, the sexuality of her breasts. "Why be so diffident? If you love me then why not simply say so?"

And if he wanted her the same. He had enjoyed her in the past and could again—the appetite she had spoken of was obviously still unappeased. But it was her appetite, not his. As always after working he felt drained.

"Ursula—"

"Don't say it!" Her hand rose to touch his lips. "I understand. We have been close too long for me to take offense. You were concerned about me and the question slipped out and how could you avoid the answer? And I?" She shrugged and turned from him to pace the floor, her sandals making small, firm noises, the echoes from the chimes turning into explosive chords. "I'm bored," she said, coming to a halt. "Bored."

"You could find diversion."

"What?" She waited as he thought, spoke as he blinked. "Well? What do you suggest? Gorion's project for landscaping the southern slopes? Sagittinia and her mobiles? Mitgang's hunt? Belzdek's drums? Debayo and his hopes of contacting the dead?"

"There's—"

"Don't bother. I know them all as well as you do." The chimes caught the pad of her sandals and turned them into melodious tinklings. "And don't suggest I take up painting. Or building. Or manufacturing perfumes. Or—" She broke off, looking at her clenched hands, the knuckles a pale azure beneath the tinted skin. Like a child she said, "Cornelius, what shall I do?"

"Have patience."

"Wait! Is that all you can suggest? And while waiting?" She answered her own question. "Where is your tekoa?"

Silently he gestured to where an ornate box rested on a small table set against a wall. The lid opened to reveal swollen pods brilliant yellow against the scarlet interior. Taking one she bit into it and felt its released pungency fill her mouth with tingling sweetness.

"Your first, Ursula?"

"Does it matter?" She selected another pod and slipped it into her mouth, biting, chewing it and the other to a pulp. "You will make love to me?"

"No."

"You're a fool." Chewing she moved toward the window and stood before the high, arched opening which framed the vista beyond. A third pod followed the others to fill her mouth and to muffle her voice. "A fool," she said again. "Why refuse when it means so little?"

But already the refusal was a thing of the past and the rejection of no importance. Nothing, now, was of importance. Not her irritation, her boredom, her lack of diversion, the cramped routine of monotonous days. All were lost in the soft mantle of the euphoria which enveloped her with memories of sweet pungency.

She felt nothing as Cornelius guided her to a chair, saw nothing as he turned it to save her eyes from the glare of the setting sun, heard nothing as he left the room and gave her over to darkness and dreams.

From the shadows the voice was a plaintive wail, "Mister, please help me. For the love of God give me food. I starve!"

Dumarest walked on, keeping to the roadside edge of the sidewalk, giving the shrouded mouth of the alley no more than a single glance. Someone lurked inside and he saw a lifted hand, a pale, strained face, eyes which held desperation. A girl barely more than a child, dressed in rags, cheeks sunken, hair a mess, naked feet crusted with sores. An object of pity but on Juba things were not always what they seemed. The girl need not be alone. A pimp could be crouching behind her in the shadows poised to rise, to strike, willing to kill in order to rob. The girl herself could be a predator offering herself as bait or she need not be a girl at all but a youth acting the part.

"Mister, please! Food for my baby! My body for a crust!"

The voice grew ugly and snarled an obscene curse as Dumarest moved on. He ignored it as he had the plea; to yield to anger and seek revenge would be to run into a trap if the beggar were other than what she seemed.

"Mister!" A harlot this time, tall, thin, her face masked with paint, perfume enveloping her like a cloud. The figure hugged by glistening plastic was lush and firm but her mouth matched the hardness of her eyes. "You lost? Lonely, maybe?"

"Lost."

"Looking for something?" Her voice was suggestive. "A game? A girl?"

"The field."

"You won't find it in the Maze." Her voice held mockery. "Drugs, yes, debauchery and degenerates if that's what you want, drink and all manner of dubious delights. But the field, no." She blinked at the coin he slipped into her hand. "What's this for?"

"An entertainer should be paid."

"An entertainer? But I'm a—" She broke off, laughing. "So I'm an entertainer."

"And one with a way with words." He smiled as she searched his face with her eyes. "And I could use a guide." He added a second coin to the first. "Which way to the field?"

"Straight ahead, third right, bear left, aim for the pylon and turn sharp left when you reach the fountain." She hefted the coins in her palm. "For as much again you could have me for what's left of the night."

"Thank you, no."

"I'm safe, mister. No hidden pimp or spiked drinks at my place. No?" Her sigh of regret was genuine. "A pity. Well, good luck—and watch yourself."

A warning which applied to all worlds but which had special meaning on Juba. A planet circling a sullen red giant hugging the fringe of the Rift. One exploited by entrepreneurs for the minerals they ripped from the soil. The dumping ground of criminals, the culture a seething mess of opposed interests. The rich lived in safe, strong houses set high on the hills surrounding the field. The merchants and traders used hotels and areas patrolled by armed and watchful guards. The poor rotted in hovels, working, starving, dying to be flung into the mud. The Maze was a vicious playground in which there was no law other than that of the jungle. A festering sore in which only the strong could hope to survive.

"No!"

Dumarest heard the cry as he neared the fountain and he halted, listening, eyes searching the area. Light came from scattered lanterns; floods of lambent color cast by bulbs set behind tinted panes the swaths of brightness edged with somber shadows. The fountain itself depicted three interwound figures locked in a suggestive embrace, the water rising from their juxtaposition spraying into an umbrella which fell with muted tinklings.

"No! Please, no!"

The voice again, strained, echoing its fear and terror. A high voice accompanied by the sudden pad of running feet. A quick, hard tattoo which came from beyond the fountain.

"Feld!"

A deeper voice which snapped a name and more footsteps, wider spaced and yet as hurried, which carried a man around the bulk of the fountain toward where Dumarest stood. Light rested between them, a patch of emerald which showed a peaked face with sunken eyes and a mouth which gaped above a ruff of beard. The hands, lifted, held a net and the belt hugging the waist supported a club.

A man hurrying to cut off another's escape. A woman, from the sound of the voice and the rapidity of the footsteps. Another, at least, would be following her and there could be more. Hunters after easy prey. Vultures avid to peck flesh and bone, to strip, to use, perhaps to kill and certain to maim.

"Feld!"

The running man checked as Dumarest called his name, halting to turn, frowning, the net lifting high as Dumarest lunged forward, his right hand weighed with the knife he had lifted from his boot. Nine inches of honed and pointed steel which flashed green in the light as it lifted to slash at the net the man threw at him, to drop, to lift again as the bearded mouth opened to yell. Before the alarm could be given the point had driven up beneath the jaw, pinning it to the palate, driving higher to crash through the sinus cavities and come to rest in the brain.

"Feld!" The deep voice, urgent now. "Hurry, damn you! Get her!"

Dumarest turned, tearing free the knife as the rapid tattoo of footsteps came to a sudden halt. Backed as she was by an umber glow he could see nothing but a shape haloed with a fuzz of hair, a hand lifted as if in mute appeal, a body which cringed as he moved toward it.

"No! Dear God, no!"

"Feld?" The deep voice snarled its impatience. "What the hell are you waiting for?"

He came from behind the woman, tall, massive, a round head set like a ball on a thickly columnar neck. The skull was coated with bristle and the ears flared in a fashion which would have been comical had he not radiated an aura of primeval savagery. He was not alone. Beside him, gliding on padded feet, was a creature almost as tall as a man, furred, high-pointed ears cocked over a sloping skull. The mouth, gaping, held pointed incisors. A mutant, the product of wild radiations which had twisted normal genes and resulted in something from nightmare. A freak but a dangerous one; Dumarest caught the gleam of retractable claws as the thing lifted its hands.

To the woman, not looking at her, Dumarest said, "There is a dead man behind me. He has a net and a club. Get to him and use them against the mutant. Move!"

If she obeyed, the furred thing would follow her, eager to prevent her escape. If she had spirit and was not totally numbed by fear she could engage its attention for long enough to give him time to settle the giant. But, in any case, the big man had to come first.

He leaned forward as Dumarest approached, scowling, one hand lifting to his waist.

"Feld? Is that you? What the hell are you playing at?"

Unless he was blind he would have recognized Dumarest for a stranger so the words were to provide a distraction. Dumarest moved as the hand lifted from the belt, closing the distance between them before the weapon it held could be brought into play. Air whined as his knife slashed upward, the edge meeting the hand at the joint of the wrist, dragging, slicing through skin and fat and tendon, releasing a shower of blood, moving on as it grated against bone.

A cut which did no more than maim, but the laser fell from the numbed fingers as the giant yelled and drew back the fist of his other arm.

And yelled again as the knife, moving upward, changed direction to slash at his eyes.

Dumarest felt the tip hit the cheek, scrape over the bone and miss the eyeball by a fraction before slicing the nose. A cut which released blood but failed to blind as he'd intended. As the knife whined on its way the cocked fist slammed forward.

As he fell Dumarest heard the woman scream.

He rolled as he landed on the cobbles, rising to dodge the vicious kick the giant aimed at his face, dodging another as he regained his feet. The blow had numbed his right shoulder and would have smashed his skull had he not risen to block it and rode the punch as it landed. A chance the big man had missed and the only one Dumarest intended he should get.

"You bastard!" The man panted as he lifted his injured wrist. "You dirty bastard!"

The hand moved as he spoke, a carmine rain spraying over Dumarest's head as he ducked and lunged, the knife a stinging extension of his arm. The giant was huge, solidly packed with muscle, resistant flesh it would be difficult to penetrate with a stab. Also he could be wearing protective clothing similar to Dumarest's own, metal mesh buried in shielding plastic and proof against point or edge.

Where was the mutant?

Had the woman screamed because it had reached her? Was it even now tearing at her throat or had she screamed to warn him of its approach?

Dumarest lunged, cut, backed as blood spurted from the inside of one of the thick thighs. Moving to one side he saw the woman, the furred shape at her side, the gleam of the claws resting against her throat. Saw, too, the laser where it lay in the street where it had fallen from the gashed hand.

He sprang, the knife lifting, moving forward as he landed, umber and emerald flashing from the blade as it left his hand. Immediately he stooped, snatched up the laser and, turning, lifted it, his finger tightening on the release as he aimed. The ruby guide beam illuminated the scarred face, added a deeper hue to the blood seeping from cheek and nose, found the eye and ruined it as the projected heat burned its way into the brain.

As the giant fell Dumarest spun, laser lifted, finger

poised on the release. His arm fell as he saw the huddled shape at the woman's feet.

"You killed it," she said blankly. "You threw something and it fell."

"A knife." He recovered it, drawing it from the throat, wiping it clean on the matted fur before thrusting it back into his boot. Are you hurt?"

"So fast," she whispered. "You moved so fast. One second you were facing that man and then, the next, you'd turned and thrown and—" She looked at her hand, at the smears on her fingers. "Blood! It tore at my throat!"

"Scratched it," corrected Dumarest. "The skin is barely broken. Why didn't you use the net and the club?"

"I tried but I couldn't seem to move fast enough. I guess I'm a coward," she admitted. "And perhaps a fool. I was warned but—" She broke off, looking at the dead. "Why did they want to hurt me?"

"For what you are and what you carry. For fun. Even, perhaps, for food. Was this yours?"

She looked at the laser he held out to her.

"Yes. I drew it when they frightened me but one knocked it from my hand. Then I ran but they followed. If it hadn't been for you I would have been helpless." She shivered then said, "Please, will you take me home?"

Chapter Two

Her name was Sardia del Naeem and she lived in a small and luxurious apartment set on the slope of a hill in an area graced with flowering trees. A safe and protected place but not her home. That was on Tonge and she had come to Juba on business. Things she told Dumarest when preparing him a drink. Vanishing into the bathroom when he took it not so much, he guessed to remove the grime of the day as to lave away the recent contact with vileness.

"Earl!" Her voice rose above the gush of the shower. "When you said those men could have been after food—did you mean it?"

"Yes."

"Literally?" The roar of water died, her voice loud and strained in the contrasting silence. "To hunt and kill their own kind as if they hunted an animal?"

He said dryly, "Have you no slums on Tonge?"

"Slums, yes, but—"

"No desperate? No starving?"

"Perhaps, but nothing like the Maze. Surely it is unique."

"No." Dumarest sipped at his drink and tasted ice and astringent bitterness. "Take a world like this and you have a place like the Maze. One with the same or a different name but one holding the same dangers. Fools go into them for amusement. The wise stay well away."

"As I should have done?"

"Yes."

"And you, Earl?"

"I was on my way to the field."

"And so saved my life." There was a click as the shower door opened. "And now, Earl, please pour me a drink."

She stepped from the bathroom as he turned, the tall glass in his hand, and they stood facing each other in the warm intimacy of the chamber. She had changed, the fuzz of hair tamed now to rest in a thick, glistening tress of shimmering jet over one rounded shoulder, the strands held by a coil of gem-set gold. Her face was oval, the eyes pools of limpid brown fringed with a fan of lashes, her skin the hue of sun-kissed olives, a brownness which held the depth of chocolate, of creamed coffee, of leaves turning from russet to umber. Her nostrils were flared a little, matching the fullness of the lips in betraying sensuality, the eyes enigmatic beneath their upswept brows. Her ears were small, the chin smoothly rounded, the neck a column of grace. Beneath a simple gown of multicolored silk her figure held the ripeness of maturity.

A woman no longer young but one who moved with the grace of a trained dancer. One who smiled as she took the proffered glass then sobered as she stared with frank appraisal at her guest.

Taller than she was by almost a head, his body hard and firm beneath the long-sleeved, high-collared tunic he wore, the smooth grey plastic marred now by minute stains. His face was hard, lines and planes presenting a mask of iron determination, the mouth alone touched with sensitivity yet one which could easily become cruel. A man who had long since learned to live alone, to rely on no one but himself.

Would he, if starving, eat what came to hand?

"My lady, is the drink not to your liking?"

"Of course." She blinked and sipped aware of the

path her thoughts had taken. One guided by his presence, the aura of masculinity he radiated and to which she felt herself respond. "Help yourself to another drink if you want."

She watched as he crossed to the table and added ice and water to the glass in his hand. It was hard to remember that only a short while ago he had killed; that the stains on his tunic and matching pants were dried blood, that the knife riding in one of the knee-high boots had cut and slashed and hurtled through the air to sink into yielding flesh. A knife fighter, she decided, such men knew better than to stab, and yet such men did not throw their blades. To do so would be to disarm themselves and, should the throw miss, death would be inevitable.

She said, as their eyes met, "You said you were on your way to the field. To join your ship?"

"To find one."

"To book passage?" Then, as he nodded, she added, "But why go through the Maze?"

"A shortcut." A lie, but it would serve and there was no need to explain that, in the winding streets, anyone following could be thrown off his trail. If anyone had been following. "And you?" He frowned as she told him. "To look for a man? In the Maze? At night?"

"I was stupid," she admitted. "But I was impatient to see him and I was armed and thought I could take care of myself."

"And?"

"I got lost in the alleys. I asked a man for directions—the small one called Feld. He said something obscene and touched me." Her free hand rose to her breasts. "I stepped back and drew the laser but he laughed and came toward me. I dodged and someone knocked the gun from my hand. The big man, I think. Then I ran."

And would have died had Dumarest not saved her.

He said, "You made a mistake. Once you drew the laser you should have used it."

"Killed without warning?"

"Why warn if you intend to kill? Why draw a weapon if you don't intend to use it?"

Simple rules and ones which, perhaps, governed his life, but she was used to a more gentle environment. Like a tamed dog she had bared her teeth hoping the sight would protect her, unwilling and unable to do more. A pathetic defense and useless against the predators she had met.

The things they could have done to her.

Ice tinkled in the glass as she emptied it with convulsive swallows, searching for the anodyne the alcohol would provide, meeting Dumarest's eyes as she lowered the container.

"It's over," he said quietly. "All over. Now you can forget it."

Men dead, blood spraying, the touch of claws at her throat. The thought of what could have happened—forget it?

Numbing she took the refilled glass Dumarest handed to her and drank and lowered it half-empty and then took a deep, shuddering breath. Was she a girl to be so afraid? A young and silly creature finding refuge in hysteria? Amil had died in her arms after his greatest performance, his heart bursting beneath the strain, blood seeping from between his lips, marring their last kiss. And Verecunda, after the leap, when she had fallen so badly and all had heard the ghastly splinter of bone—no, she was not a child!

Dumarest said, "Better now?"

"You think I am weak?"

"No, a woman who is human."

"A fool?"

"A person." He set down his own glass. "Is there anything I can do for you before I leave."

"Leave?"

He said, patiently, "You are home now. Safe. Take something if you must but don't dwell on the past. It's over. Finished. Just forget it."

"You keep saying that. Do you think it so easy?"

"No," he admitted. "But sometimes it needs to be done." Then, as she made no comment, he added, "Do you need medical assistance? The shock—"

"Is one I can handle. She inhaled, inflating her chest, automatically throwing back her shoulders and tightening her stomach. Rising on her points she spun in a graceful pirouette then crossed the floor to where a cube glowed in kaleidoscopic shimmers. As she touched it the shifting rainbows stilled and music softly filled the air.

"Poisanard's Suite," she said. "You know it?"

"No."

"It's quite recent, the last thing he ever did. He composed it a month before he died. Some say that it holds the sum total of his life, but I disagree. He was too boisterous for that. He lived and, having lived, moved on. The music holds what is to come not what has gone. Listen and you will appreciate what I mean."

Listen for how long? And, while listening, what would he lose? From the window Dumarest could see the distant field, the ring of lights around the perimeter fence bright against the clouded sky. Even as he watched a ship lifted, seeming to hang poised for a moment, a shimmering bubble which darted upward wreathed in its Erhaft field, to dwindle, to vanish as it drove into space.

A ship he had missed because a woman had chosen to walk into danger.

A passage lost because of a coincidental meeting.

It had to be that. There had been no way of telling which route he would take or the time he would take it. The woman, as far as he could tell, was genuine and there had been nothing contrived about the way those who had accosted her had died.

His eyes shifted focus, looked at her reflection on the pane, the smooth, olive features, the eyes which looked into distance and not at his back. An intelligent woman—too intelligent to risk walking the Maze at night unless driven by a desperate need. Or perhaps she was simply ignorant—Tonge was not Juba and those accustomed to gentle worlds found it hard to accept the savagery normal on harsher planets.

Without turning he said, "What are you?"

"A dancer."

"A what?"

"A dancer. Ballet. On Tonge I was the prima ballerina of the Corps Mantage. You have seen ballet? You know something of it? A harsh discipline, Earl, and endless exercise. It takes skill and stamina and suppleness. It takes time and dedication. And then—" She shrugged and gestured, hands fluttering like pale moths against the pane. "I grew old. It is as simple as that."

"And came to Juba." He turned and stared into her eyes. "To dance?"

"To deal. When you are old in ballet, Earl, you are finished. Continue too long and bones grow brittle, sinews lose their elasticity and applause turns into derision. Now I deal in works of art. With luck fortunes can be made."

"How?"

"Not by finding rare and costly treasures, Earl, though that, too, at times. No, the thing is to find an artist who has yet to be appreciated. To buy his work cheap and then to sell it dear. To hold it, build his reputation, to display it, have it enhanced by select critical praise, then to cash in on the created demand."

"To rob," said Dumarest. "To pay the artist a pittance and then to make a pile. And you call the Maze a jungle?"

"It isn't the same," she protested. "A work of art is valueless until it has found a buyer. And once the artist is known he will get his reward. Once he is known," she added bitterly. "Once he is found. That's why I was in the Maze. To find a man who might know a man who—but why go on? It's hopeless."

"The prima ballerina of the Corps Mantage," said Dumarest softly. "Yet once you were a small girl leaning on a barre and trying to stand on your points. Did you think it was hopeless then? A waste of time even to try?"

"This is different. Have you ever looked for a needle in a haystack?"

Looked and was looking, but he said nothing of his search for the world of his birth.

"You must have clues, Sardia. The artist, for instance, you must have samples of his work. It is a man?"

"I don't know, Earl. It could be a man or a woman but I think it likely to be a man. A matter of instinct, I'll admit, and I could be wrong." Rising from where she sat she stilled the music and poured them both fresh drinks. Handing a glass to Dumarest she continued, "I'm following a rainbow and hoping for a pot of gold. Some paintings were offered to a gallery on Tonge and I was fortunate enough to be the one approached. I was an associate, but never mind that, the thing is I recognized the genius of their creator. Naturally I wanted to know more but the vendor could only tell me he'd bought them from a man on Juba. Someone here, in this city, who owns a shop close to the field. I saw him and he claimed ignorance of the origin of the paintings. I tried a little bribery and gained the address of a man who worked for the dealer at times. He lives in the Maze. I went to find him—the rest you know."

"How long have you been on Juba?"

"A couple of weeks. This place is rented. Why?"

"Two weeks. Did it take you that long to find the local dealer?"

"He was away and it took time to check him out. I

had to scour the galleries and find out what I could before I approached him."

"And?"

"He admitted nothing, but that's normal, he'd want to retain his source of supply. Naturally I was casual in my approach. I acted the part of a tourist looking for an interesting souvenir. Luckily he had two parts of a triptych and I asked for the address of the artist so as to obtain the third. He wouldn't give it to me. The artist, naturally, wasn't the one I am looking for but it shows the man's caution. I'd hoped to learn more from his assistant."

And had failed and had almost lost her life and lacked the courage to try again. But Dumarest?

She said thoughtfully, "You could help me, Earl."

"No."

"Please." His refusal increased her desire to gain his aid. "I need you to help me. All it will take is a little time. You are accustomed to dealing with men like the dealer. He will respect you. And once we find the artist I promise you will not regret it. A share of what I make. A third of the clear profit."

"No."

"How much then? A half? A half of all we make, Earl. Equal partnership. I'll advance all expenses which will later be deducted." Hesitating, she added, "This agreement to be for the first items obtained. I—why do you smile?"

"As a dancer, Sardia, you make a good dealer."

"I am a dealer, and when you work for the Corps Mantage you learn to keep your wits about you. A deal, Earl?"

"No."

"But why not? Can't you spare the time? Don't you trust me?" Her voice hardened a little. "Is that it? Do you think I've been feeding you a pack of lies."

"Not lies, Sardia. But perhaps a dream."

"The coordinates of the world of solid treasure. The

clue to a fabulous fortune. The whereabouts of Bonanza, maybe, or El Dorado, or Jackpot, Avalon or even Earth. I've heard them all before. Men who try to cash in on ignorance or greed or who try to buy favors with a list of figures. Fools for trying it and bigger fools for thinking others can be so gullible. But I'm not trying to sell you a legend, Earl. Not the location of some mythical planet. My artist is real and I can prove it!"

She vanished into a room which held a bed, reappeared holding a canvas which she thrust toward him. "Here!"

The painting was that of a child crying, and the artist had caught all the pain and torment of the universe in the young and innocent face.

"It's good," said Dumarest.

"Good? It's superb! Look at it, damn you! *Look* at it!"

A thing of ten by twenty inches, the background dark, the central figure luminated by a glowing, mottled ball. The child dressed in a nondescript gown so that it could have been of either sex. The face round, the eyes luminous, liquid with tears which fell over the cheeks, the little hands clenched, one holding a thorned rose, the other a tattered thing of rag and buttons. A doll which had given pleasure as the flower had given pain. On the hand gripping it, touches of red showed where blood had seeped from wounds caused by the thorns. Pleasure and pain—the summation of existence.

"Look at the detail," whispered the woman. "Study it. You can see every thread, every stitch, every grain of the sand on which the child is sitting. You can almost smell the scent of the rose. You can almost feel the pain of the thorns. Look at it, sink into it, feel it—Earl, feel it, man! Feel it!"

And, suddenly, he was a child again sitting on a harsh and barren slope with the bitter wind stinging his eyes and filling them with tears, while, in his hand, the small creature he had caught squirmed and wriggled and fought for its life as he was fighting for his. The lizard he would shortly eat, biting it, chewing, swallowing it raw. Life dying to maintain life. Savagery beneath the moon.

The moon?

"Earl!" The woman touched his hand. "Earl?"

He ignored her, eyes focused on the mottled ball illuminating the crying child. A rough, pitted, scarred and cratered orb depicted with the same painstaking detail as the garment, the sand, the doll, the rose and the thorn. A ball which bore the semblance of a skull. One he had seen before.

"Earl?" Sardia's fingers were warm against his own. "Earl, is anything wrong?"

Again he ignored her, lifting the painting, tilting it, his eyes hungry as they examined the silvery ball. A full moon. A familiar sight.

The moon he had seen when a child on earth.

There was money on Juba. The minerals torn from far below the surface, shipped, provided a steady stream of wealth reflected in the luxurious appointments of the houses set high on the hills but those who owned the most displayed it the least. On Juba only the children were close to the Cyclan.

Cyber Hine studied them as he stood behind the door leading to the classroom. The one-way glass gave him a clear view and he watched with calm detachment as Necho turned in his seat to whisper to Baaras behind, to Ceram at one side. A restless boy and yet one who showed promise. A useful addition if his questing nature could be brought under control and, in any case, a future supporter of the institution which now gave him food, accommodation and education. A debt which, later, he would repay.

"Master!" The acolyte was looking at him and Hine examined the smooth face for any sign of disrespect. A man older than himself, one who had failed to reach the required degree as yet, but one who would continue to try and continue to serve. "It is time, Master," he said. "The pupils are waiting."

And could wait and would wait should he so decide, but Hine was aware of his recently enhanced status and the fact that, in a sense, he was on probation. How he acted, how he conducted himself, all were of importance to future advancement and the acolyte, as was proper, would report as to his attitude.

A nod and the door was opened, the whispers dying as the tall figure in the scarlet robe swept into the room to take his place on the podium. From his elevated position Hine stared at the class, his face impassive, his shaven head adding to his skull-like appearance. A *cyber* was never fat; excess tissue was wasteful in terms of energy consumption and proof that the diet was ill-balanced in relation to need. Food was fuel, the body a mechanism to house the brain, the brain itself the seat of the all-important intelligence. What impaired the efficiency of the mind was bad, what aided it was good—a dictum which determined how a *cyber* was dressed, how he lived, even the very temperature of his environment.

"You will pay attention," said Hine. "During this session we shall be concerned with logical extrapolation of sequences. On the screen before you will be flashed a picture consisting of twenty-three shapes. From the others shown at the foot of the panel you must select the one which belongs to the set of twenty-four. Commence."

A simple exercise but one designed both to stimulate the mind and to signal potential material for higher and more selective training. It was followed by others, each a little harder than those previously given, the inbuilt desk computer keeping the scores. It was low and Hine pressed a button on the master panel to scramble and repeat the sequence on the same basic level as before but with different images.

"A warning," said Hine, his voice maintaining its even modulation: a tone devoid of any irritant factors.

"If you fail this time then an electric shock will be given. The intensity will increase in ratio to continued failure."

A whip to drive them to better effort and the reward of food later for those who passed a determined level. Hine sat, light reflecting from the design on the breast of his scarlet robe, the Seal of the Cyclan which, in time, some of those now studying could wear. Would wear if previous experience was of any value. Must wear if the Cyclan was to expand and survive.

Sitting, watching, his face impassive Hine remembered his own past and training. The sons of the wealthy and influential, while educated, were rarely selected to wear the scarlet robe. There was no need; conditioned, they would serve the aims of the Cyclan when it came to them to adopt the trappings of power. Others, those with ambitious parents, had their minds sharpened and their sympathies directed so that they, too, became invisible extensions of the vast organization. From the poor, the desperate, the hungry, came those who sought to rule the entire galaxy.

The *cybers* who wore the scarlet robe.

The living machines of flesh and blood dedicated to the pursuit of total and absolute domination of all living things in the universe.

Servants of the Cyclan of which Hine was one.

He had been starving, covered with sores, rotten with a wasting disease and willing to do anything for a bowl of soup or a crust of bread. Insanity had driven him to attempt to steal from a *cyber*, careless of the dire penalties which all knew befell those caught. And he had been caught—even now he could remember the terror which had engulfed him at the thought of being turned into a living horror, his limbs distorted, amputated, grafted into new positions on his body so that he would walk backward and upside down—fears born of whispers which peopled the unknown with nightmare.

Instead he had been washed and fed and tested. And

healed and taught and tested. And watched and probed and tested again and again by those for whom such work was a specialty. Food had become something to be taken without enjoyment and without thought as to its source. Emotions were to be controlled, diminished, negated. The mind was paramount at all times at any cost. The body was a machine.

Of his class some vanished without explanation. Others were punished with merciless application. A few reached a desired proficiency.

At puberty he was operated on; an adjustment to the cortex which took from him the ability to feel emotion. Never would he know hate or love, hope or fear, joy or despair. Freed of the hampering effect of such disturbing afflictions he could concentrate solely on the expansion of his mind and the trained talent he possessed. One which gave the Cyclan its awesome power.

"Necho, come here." The boy had scored high. Now Hine gestured to the shapes lying before him. "One is different from the others. Which?"

A boy, awed, would spend long minutes looking for the difference which he couldn't see, too timid to accuse his master of deception. Another would find a difference where none existed; doubting his own judgment.

Necho said, "Master, they are the same."

Silently Hine reached out and turned the pieces over. One held an indentation.

"Master, I thought—"

"You assumed," corrected Hine. "You did not listen or, listening, you failed to understand. Twelve strokes of the birch will impress the lesson on your memory. That and going foodless to bed."

A harsh punishment, but a good tool needed to be tempered. One day, perhaps, the boy would become an acolyte and even be elevated to a *cyber*. Once accepted, there was no limit as to how high he could rise. Given time he could become the *Cyber* Prime himself and certainly, if proven worthy, he would end as a unit of Central Intelligence.

As would all who wore the Seal.

The reward of a lifetime of service when, the body failing, the brain would be removed from the skull and immersed in a vat of nutrient fluids. There, in series with countless others, it would live on, aware, conscious, working to solve problem after problem until the smallest secret and the largest had been made clear. Until all things were united into a common whole.

The aim and object of the Cyclan.

Higher in the building *Cyber* Buis sat neither brooding nor permitting himself the indulgence of memory. Such things were the natural irritations of youth, and between himself and Hine stretched half a century of dedicated effort. Time enough for him to have climbed to the summit of the Cyclan on Juba and more than time for him to have sharpened his talent to the fine point of keenness which gave its own reward in terms of mental achievement. The only true pleasure any *cyber* could know aside from the heady intoxication of communication with Central Intelligence.

A time when the engrafted Homochon elements would be stimulated by the Samatachazi formulae and mental contact achieved with the tremendous complex lying at the heart of the headquarters of the Cyclan. A form of near-instantaneous mental transmission which bridged the gulf between the stars and made all *cybers* basically one.

But such communication was used only as a necessity aside from the regular schedules and there was other work to be done. Buis glanced at the sheaf of reports lying on his desk, flipping papers as each was scanned, its content assessed, correlated, intermeshed with the whole. Others would have filtered the data but still the sheaf was thick, for who could ever be certain that

INCIDENT ON ATH

some minor detail, some apparent trifle might not hold the key to a far more complex situation.

A button sank beneath his finger as Buis spoke into a recorder.

"Action on report 354782. Manufacture of synthetic drug HXT 239Z to be discontinued. Hints to be spread of mutations discovered in Jelman's Sickness. New drug HXT 5Y to be introduced as a substitute for that withdrawn."

At double the price and the bankruptcy of the plant packaging the discontinued compound. Another would get the contract and the Cyclan would gain not only wealth but a grateful client. And, as a bonus, a lesson would have been taught to those who opposed accepting the services of the Cyclan and the advice the *cybers* gave.

A small victory, perhaps, but battles were won because of small victories and, with the battles, the war.

Another sheet, a decision, another, a momentary hesitation as Buis assimilated the information it contained. Data apparently unrelated to another problem but facts which filled a gap. Mentally he reviewed the situation, building from a known base, extrapolating the logical sequence of events, selecting those of the highest order of probability and arriving at a prediction which was as certain as anything could be in a universe afflicted by unknown factors.

His talent, the ability of every *cyber*, the skill of being able to take a handful of facts and, from them, extrapolate what most likely would take place. The service offered to those in high places where decisions needed to be made. To those in industry who had to gain knowledge of market trends. To politicians and rulers and those who aspired to power. The subtle, unseen, hidden power which guided the destiny of worlds as if they had been puppets on a string.

More sheets, scanned, put by; situations which could

wait, others developing as planned, items of no relevant interest. Then one which caught his attention.

Into a communicator Buis said, "Mharle, with reference to report 382534. A client requesting computer time at the Cha'Nang Institute. One concerned with spectroscopic determination."

A moment then, "I have it. In view of the general directive I judged it best to refer the matter to you."

"As you should. The report gives no name."

"None was given."

"Elaborate."

"It was a simple inquiry as to available computer time as appertaining to a stellar search to match an existing spectrogram. The information given was, of necessity, of a general nature such as cost per minute of use of installation and the probability of narrowing the search by eliminating obviously unsuitable stars. The usual fee for such initial inquiries was paid. The inquiry was not unusual in the light of the commerce attached to Juba. Only the general directive made it significant."

"No name? No address?"

"No."

"And, of course, no description? As I expected." Buis's voice carried no hint of irritation but mentally he made a note to reassess Mharle's standing. The man had overlooked the obvious. While it was true that a port with heavy traffic could expect such inquiries yet they would originate from shipping companies or from captains owning their own vessels. Neither would make idle investigations. And neither would fail to have registered their names so as to offset the initial fee against the cost of any later search.

A civilian then, one cautiously feeling his way, content to pay for limited information.

One caught by the general directive which had been designed to do just that.

No, not caught, not yet. One isolated and centered in aroused interest. A target. Quarry to be hunted down.

"Master?" Mharle was waiting.

"Have men wait at the Cha'Nang Institute. Continuous surveillance. If anyone makes similar inquiries have them followed and, if they attempt to leave the city, apprehended. Use any force necessary but, under no circumstances is the life of the subject to be endangered. Set a similar watch at the field. Description as on directive ED 201. Orders as above. Apprehend but do not endanger. And, Mharle—do not fail."

Buis looked at his hand as it fell from the button of the communicator. It was thin, thickly veined, the skin mottled, the fingers claw-like with age. A long life and a busy one in which he had served the Cyclan with every cell of his being. And now, at the end—he watched as his hand closed as if gripping something of inestimable value.

Dumarest on Juba!

It had to be Dumarest. A man, making such an inquiry, taking such precautions—who else could it be?

One who had, somehow, slipped through the net set to catch him after his whereabouts had been determined on a distant world. The attempt made there to gain information as to the whereabouts of a certain star repeated here. The same interest in the spectrum of a forgotten sun. The man the Cyclan searched for. The man they needed to find.

The secret they had to regain.

Leaning back Buis closed his eyes, reliving the time when, in communication with Central Intelligence, all had been made clear to him. A discovery stolen from a secret laboratory of the Cyclan and passed on to Dumarest. The affinity twin which could give one mind the power to enter the body of a prepared host and dominate it. To become that actual person. To feel and see and walk and talk and live in a new body. A means to dominate the rich and powerful, to use them with *cyber* minds controlling their bodies, to extend the rule and power of the Cyclan to every inhabited star.

A universe held in a molecular chain of fifteen biochemical units, one of which, reversed, determined the subjective or dominant characteristics. The biochemical units were known. What the affinity twin could do had been demonstrated.

But the correct order in which the fifteen units had to be assembled was the secret Dumarest carried in his brain.

One which would be rediscovered given time—but the possible combinations ran into millions. If a chain could be formed and tested every second, still it would take millennia to test them all. Endless years which the capture of one man could save.

Dumarest!

Buis opened his eyes and looked at his hand now closed tighter than before. Dumarest was on Juba—he was certain of it. It was only a matter of time before he was found.

Chapter Three

She was soft and warm and moistly engulfing. A creature of passion and demanding heat with skin like silk and curves which united into a symphony of delight. Her odor was enticing; that of rain-drenched loam, of sun-kissed grain, of an opening bud, the scent rising from the milk-dappled lips of a child. And, even when sprawled in satiated abandon, she held a lithe and lovely grace.

A dancer and now a dealer she had told him—*but what else?*

Lifting himself on one elbow Dumarest looked down at the woman in the pale light of a breaking dawn. Asleep she was more beautiful than awake, small tensions eased, muscles relaxed, the hand of time lifted from brow and cheek and the corners of the eyes. The mane of her loosened hair lay like a serpent over the pillow, the naked roundness of a shoulder, the proud mound of a breast. In her throat, beneath the rich olive of her skin, a small pulse beat like a tiny drum. Below it lay the carotid artery—a pressure and she would fall from sleep into unconsciousness and if the pressure were maintained, into soft and easy death.

"Earl!" Turning she muttered his name, head moving to present her lips, her eyes, the lashes which lay like nighted moths on her cheeks. "Earl!"

A dream in which, perhaps, she was again lost in passionate abandon.

Gently he rose and moved into the kitchen, heating coffee and taking it into the living room where, again, he searched the furnishings with his eyes. The apartment was what she had claimed it to be, a place rented for a limited stay, the appointments a standard necessity. Only the music cube was hers. That and a delicate vase of striated crystal, a framed portrait of an elderly man—her father perhaps—a scrap of embroidered silk, her clothes, her cosmetics, the painting of a crying child.

The painting which depicted a moon bearing the semblance of a skull.

Again Dumarest studied it, holding it to the window, using a glass to magnify detail. Was it what he hoped or had memory played tricks? A combination of light and shadow, a silver hue, a desperate yearning—a combination loaded with potential danger. As was the woman herself.

Logic told him that she had to be what she claimed but the instinct which had saved him so often before refused to permit him to lower his guard. The attack could, despite his previous conviction, have been the prelude to a trap. One baited with warm and yielding flesh. With the painting of the child. A snare which could snap shut at any moment.

"Earl?" Sardia was awake, calling sleepily from the bed. "Earl, where are you?"

"Here."

"Why are you up?" Her voice grew sharper. "Is anything wrong?"

"No. I wanted some coffee. A moment and I'll bring you some."

"I felt you missing," she said, her voice regaining its first softness. "Even though asleep I sensed you had left me."

Like an animal sensing danger. As if he had woken

during the night to lie listening to her movements as she searched his garments, saying nothing, doing nothing, acting the part of a man lost in dreams. Now he checked his clothes, finding all intact, his fingers lingering on the belt and the hilt of the knife.

"Earl?"

"Coming." He returned to the kitchen, poured coffee, entered the bedroom with steaming cups in his hands. Offering her one he looked down at the beauty revealed as she sat upright. "You slept well?"

"Like a child, Earl. Like a woman in love who lies with her lover. And you?"

"The same."

A lie to match her own and one given for the same reason perhaps. Only a fool would take a stranger on trust and in the sanity following the idiocy of passion native caution could have prevailed. An attribute he could respect.

"Earl?"

"It's time to get to work." He set down his cup and stepped into the shower, washing, drying himself, dressing as she finished the last of her coffee. "You're sure as to the address?"

"It was the one given me. You think it false?"

"It's there."

"But the man isn't." She set aside her cup with sudden irritation. "A day now and no progress. Earl, is there nothing I can do?"

"You sit here and you wait," he said flatly. "As you did yesterday. At times I may have to call you."

Again as he had done yesterday, finding her home each time, inventing some reason for the call. At least it pinned her down and, if she tried to call out, she would find the phone useless—a thing Dumarest had arranged.

Now she said, "Earl, how long?"

"Days perhaps. A month, even." He was deliberately pessimistic. "Does it matter?"

"It matters. I—" She broke off and shrugged. "Forget it. Just do your best but, please, Earl, waste no time. Others could be on the hunt and we may arrive late if at all. I'd hate to hear the artist has been spirited away or all his future work placed under contract." She slipped from the bed, a living statue of femininity darkly enticing against the snowy expanse of the sheets. "Good luck, darling." Her arms closed around his neck and pulled his lips to hers. "And don't keep me waiting too long."

At night the Maze held a glamor, a dangerous one, perhaps, but one which gilded with a tinsel sheen the dirt and neglect of moldering buildings, the filth accumulated in the streets which only the rains washed away. By day it held the appearance of an aging harlot, waking, her paint cracked, the raddled features showing through. And, like such a creature, the place had a smell.

To Dumarest it was familiar; the odor of rancid grease, of must, of rot, of damp and sickness, the whole overlaid by the indefinable but unmistakable stench of poverty. A smell prevalent in all Lowtowns where the abandoned and desperate huddled in a common misery and one which had found a place in this man-made jungle.

"Brother! Of your charity!"

The monk was a brave man but all who had dedicated their lives to the Universal Church had courage. Dumarest looked at the empty bowl of chipped plastic the man held before him, his eyes lifting to study the brown homespun robe, the seamed face shadowed by the cowl. Beneath the hem of the rough garment the feet were bare in crude sandals.

"You are out early, Brother."

"Misery does not sleep." The bowl lifted a little. "And starvation does not wait." The voice cracked a little as Dumarest poured coins into the bowl. "Brother, you are generous!"

"You have a church in the Maze?"

"Not in the Maze. At the field."

A small place fashioned of poles and plastic sheeting holding little more than a chair for the monk, a place for the suppliant, the Benediction light which stood between them. The light at which the suppliant would stare as he confessed his sins and asked forgiveness. Absolution would be granted after which the worshipper, after subjective penance, would be hypnotically conditioned against the ability to kill.

A fair exchange for the wafer of concentrates which was given as the bread of forgiveness and which many only came to the church to obtain. But, if with it they could absorb the basic credo of the Universal Brotherhood, the monks were content.

There, but for the grace of God, go I!

Once all men could look at their fellows and remember that the millennium would have arrived.

"Brother, you are cold." Dumarest had seen the shiver which had gripped the old man. "Here." He added more coins to those in the bowl. "This is for you. Get something hot to eat and drink."

"I collect for charity."

"Charity begins at home. If you fall ill who will take your place?" An empty question; another would follow and after him yet more. Humble men trying in their own way to lift the burden of misery afflicting the majority. But, though humble, they possessed an iron resolution. As the monk looked at his bowl Dumarest said, "You could help me, Brother. Have you noticed strangers hanging about this vicinity? Men who do not belong yet who wait?"

The old eyes moved in their sockets as they studied Dumarest's face.

"You intend harm to another?"

"No, but there are those who are not my friends. I would prefer not to meet them."

"And you think they are close?" The monk pursed his lips as Dumarest nodded, his eyes veiled, thoughtful. Abruptly he said, "Here you have nothing to fear. No strangers lurk in the Maze. But there are men at the field who do nothing but watch and others wait at the premises of the Cha'Nang."

Men poised and ready to strike. Dumarest's face hardened as he walked on down the narrow street. His instinct had not lied—the trap he had sensed was real and was closing. A snare he could have eluded had he taken ship when he'd first intended. A passage he would have gained and he would now be far into the void if it hadn't been for Sardia and her painting. Time wasted in pursuit of a dream.

More time wasted as he hammered at a sagging door set with a thickly barred Judas grill.

Yesterday it had remained closed; now it opened with a grate of rusty hinges to reveal a scowling, bearded face.

"You want something?"

"Eprius Emecheta—that you?"

"And if it is?"

"We have business." Dumarest smiled and winked. "Open up, man. It's worth five durinne to listen."

"Five? Make it ten."

"Five." Dumarest showed the coins. "Just for a little talk and maybe a drink. You've something in the house?"

"This ain't no tavern, mister. You want something to drink then you pay for it. Make it ten and I'll open up."

Money changed hands as Dumarest stepped through the opened portal into a passage reeking of staleness. The room opening from it held a sagging bed, a table littered with stained crockery, scraps of food, odorous cartons. A rat scuttled as they entered to stare warily from beneath the bed. Stains crawled on the walls: vermin seeking shadowed safety.

A nest—its occupant as much vermin as the things crawling on the walls.

"Wine." Emecheta tilted a dusty bottle. "Here."

The glass was cracked, chipped, slimed with grease and the wine matched the container. Dumarest sipped and tasted a sour roughness then, conscious of the other's suspicious stare, swallowed and held out the empty glass.

"More?"

"I've paid for it." His tone was deliberately hostile; a man like Emecheta would take common politeness for weakness. "Give!"

Again he sipped and watched as his host gulped at his own glass. A squat, hairy man, his chest a mat of greasy darkness, the backs of his hands bearing a curly growth. Beneath bristling brows his eyes were the watchful orbs of an animal.

"Well?"

"Word has it that you're a man who likes to make a little easy money," said Dumarest. "That gives us something in common. I move around and at times pick up a few things of value. The trouble is selling them. People ask questions, you know?" His wink was expressive. "Now if I had a partner who had an outlet . . . ?" He fell silent then said harshly, "Do I have to spell it out?"

"I'm no fence."

"Did I say you were?" Dumarest finished his wine and reached for the bottle topping up both glasses. "And did I say I was a thief? I'm talking about stuff sneaked from the field. Hell, man, are you dumb? They told me you were smart."

"Who told you that?"

"People who figured to do me a favor. You, too. There's a hundred durinne in it, maybe. Easy pickings, but it seems I'm wasting my time." Dumarest picked up his wine, sipped, spat in disgust. "Let me out of here!"

"What's the hurry?" Emecheta didn't move from where he sat, but one hand had vanished from view. "Sit down and I'll open a new bottle. Decent stuff. Now just what did you have in mind?"

"First the hand," said Dumarest coldly. "I want to see it and it had better be empty." He nodded as it came into view. Now stand up and move away from the table." His hand dropped to his knee, the hilt of the knife. "Do it!"

Grunting, Emecheta obeyed, heaving up his bulk and standing against a wall, away from the wine, the table, the weapon Dumarest guessed he had concealed beneath it.

"Well?"

"We talk," said Dumarest. "About you, the people you work for, the outlets you have. And about money—but first we have some decent wine."

She answered on the second attempt. "Earl! I was getting worried. It's been so long."

"Where were you?"

"When?" She answered her own question. "Did you call earlier? I was in the shower."

A reasonable excuse but Dumarest was edgy and some of it showed. "I told you to stand by the phone. How much money can you raise?"

"Why?"

"To use, to spend, to buy things." He smoothed his tone. "You'd better meet me. Bring that music cube of yours and jewelry if you have it. I'll wait for you in the restaurant at the corner of Spacehaven and Drell. Get a cab and hurry."

He took his time joining her, watching for men who had no apparent excuse to linger, taking the chair beside her only when he was sure she hadn't come with companions.

"Earl!" Her hand closed over his, the brown fingers holding a surprising strength. "How was he?"

"Emecheta?"

"Yes. Could I have handled him?"

"You would have been raped," said Dumarest flatly. "Then you'd have been robbed. You could even have been killed."

"He's that bad?"

"He's filth." Dumarest poured himself a glass of water. "Order some food. You brought what I asked?"

"Yes. Why do you want it, Earl?"

"Later. First let us eat."

She ordered wisely, dishes high in protein and low in bulk, foods giving high energy and among the most expensive the place offered. Dumarest refused the offer of wine and finished the meal with fruit.

"Emecheta is scum," he said as they sat over coffee. "But you weren't robbed when you gained his name. The dealer you mentioned, Pude Ahdram?"

"Yes. I could have told you that, Earl, but I—"

"Couldn't trust me and didn't want me cutting in." He was brusque with his interruption. "But let's waste no more time. He deals with anyone who has items of value and does a brisk trade with those from the field. Contraband and anything which shows a profit or so Emecheta claimed. He could be lying but I don't think so. We can use him."

"How?" She blinked as he told her. "Give him my music cube and jewelry? Earl, are you serious?"

"I'll tell him I've stolen them. He'll take them to Ahdram for sale. If what he told me is true, the dealer will buy if the price is right. Then you go into his shop, quest around, ask for something unusual and keep looking until he produces the cube. Then create a fuss, tell him the cube is yours, that it was stolen with other things, talk about summoning the authorities. There's no law in the Maze but there's plenty at the field and elsewhere in town. He'll want to avoid an investigation."

"And I press him," she said slowly. "And keep on

pressing until he tells me what I want to know. The name and whereabouts of the artist. Earl—"

"Do you know a better way?"

"No," she admitted. "But I'm not sure if I can handle it. I'm not strong enough. I lack aggression. How can I, a woman, force information from a man like that?"

"You're an actress."

"No, Earl, a dancer."

"And when dancing you acted a part, right?" He lifted her hand and flexed her fingers. "And never think of yourself as weak. I've seen you, remember? Felt your strength."

Muscles like coiled springs beneath the silken olive of her skin; tissue trained and developed to meet the needs of a demanding art. The strength which had gripped him as the lissom thighs had closed, joining the restraint of her arms, her hands. A strength born of physical passion but anger could provide as good a stimulus and determination even a greater.

"We must try," he said gently. "You must try."

"And if I fail? You will help me, Earl?"

To join in the argument, to make himself conspicuous and to advertise his presence to those who watched the field and its environs. A stupidity he intended to avoid.

"If you fail we'll try something else," he promised. "Just do your best and if he doesn't play along summon the authorities and accuse him of receiving stolen goods. You can prove ownership?"

"Yes. The cube holds a thousand recordings many of which I can name in sequence. And I insured the jewelry on arrival."

"Good. Then there should be no trouble." Dumarest glanced through the windows; already it was close to noon. "We'd best hurry."

"I'll go to the shop," she decided. "Linger as if I'm a tourist killing time. When Emecheta enters I'll follow

INCIDENT ON ATH 45

him." Remembering she added, "How will I know him? We've never met."

"Squat, hairy, repulsive." Dumarest finished his coffee. "You'll know him by his smell if nothing else, but enter before he does if you can. Ahdram will be unwilling to leave you alone for long and so will be quick to settle the deal. And it might help if you primed him."

"With talk of a music cube? Leave it to me, Earl." Then, anticipating his doubt she added, smiling, "I'm a dealer, too, remember. You can't trade in items of value without learning the art of misdirection. Where shall I meet you"

"Here." He rose to his feet. "Give me an hour to meet Emecheta and pass on the goods."

"You'll be close?"

"Yes," he promised. "I'll be close."

Close enough to see the squat man waddle to the shop of Pude Ahdram eager to make an easy profit and already, no doubt, figuring out ways to cheat his mysterious partner. Close enough to have seen the woman enter shortly before, to have seen her casual approach and to have admired her skill at appearing other than what she was. Close enough to have spotted the men who stood and watched and moved only to take up fresh positions so as to watch again.

Watch and move in when their quarry had been spotted and Dumarest had no doubt as to who that was.

He turned, glancing into windows, hesitating, moving on with a calculated speed. A man who was not in a hurry, who watched no particular point, who was just an aimless traveler killing time. Yet, always, he watched the shop.

Sardia was taking her time. Twice he caught glimpses of her through the barred windows, talking, gesticulating, presenting a show of enthusiasm over some trifle, shaking her head over another. A skilled practitioner of a difficult art, that of deluding another that what was wanted was of no interest and of little worth.

A dancer turned dealer—where had she learned to lie so well?

There was time to think about it as there was time to think of other things. Of the men in scarlet who even now were predicting just where and when he would be, what he would do, what path he would take. Plotting his course with growing accuracy as his movements left traces which could be garnered and included into the common whole. *Cybers* who, given the data, could pinpoint his presence at a particular place at a particular time.

Unless he could defeat them as he had so often before.

Unless the luck which had saved him should suddenly run out.

But luck, as he never ceased to remember, came in two kinds—the bad and the good.

And now it seemed time for the bad.

It was on Sardia's face as, finally, she stepped from the shop, hands empty of her possessions. Dumarest moved quickly to remain out of sight, following her as she headed toward the rendezvous, catching her up when he was certain she had not been followed.

"Earl!" She looked up as he caught her arm. "I thought we were to meet in the restaurant."

"I changed my mind." A cab halted at his signal. "We'll go to Dekart Heights."

It was a place of scented shrubs and flowering trees, of emerald sward dotted with the fallen stars of golden blooms. A lake stretched beyond a park set with miniature pavilions graced with fretted pennants and hung with chiming bells. A place for lovers wishing to be alone. For conspirators afraid of being overheard.

"Earl!" she said as he guided her to a seat. "Oh, Earl!"

"You failed—it is written on your face."

"No, that is, I—" She calmed beneath the touch of his hand. "Luck, my darling, a coincidence, but they happen and when they do so many problems can be solved."

And so many created, but he didn't mention that.

"What happened?"

He listened as she told him, the chime of bells a delicate accompaniment to her voice. She had entered the shop as planned and, as expected, Ahdram had remembered her from her previous visit. But the man had not been alone. Another was with him with paintings for sale.

"I recognized them, Earl. The technique is unmistakable. The work of the artist I need to find."

Need? A subconscious betrayal which Dumarest noted.

"So everything was simple. You asked the man who the artist was and where to find him."

"No. As I told you things aren't done that way in the field of art. Even to admit to an interest is to arouse suspicion that the work is of higher value than previously thought."

"So?"

"I kept to our original plan. It worked up to a point but I had to wait until the stranger had left Ahdram and me alone. His greed made him show me the cube and I accused him of theft. He was distraught and offered restitution and recompense—the cunning bastard!"

Dumarest said dryly, "He found out what you wanted and offered to help—and demanded a price for his aid."

"You know?"

"I guessed. Dealers are much the same and Ahdram had to be shrewd in order to survive." An expert in a field in which she was an amateur. "The cube?"

"And the jewelry." A bracelet of ornate workmanship set with brilliant gems. "He demanded them both in return for information and I had no choice but to agree." Her hands clenched, the knuckles taut beneath the skin, the nails making small crescents in the flesh of her palms. "The swine!"

"He cheated you? He lied?"

"No," she said bitterly. "He didn't lie. The paintings were genuine and he told me how he got them. But he was playing with me—they don't come from Juba at all!"

Chapter Four

From outside the pavilion in which they sat, rising above the susurration of tinkling bells, came the sound of childish laughter and a woman's voice calling a warning. A small boy, chasing a brilliantly colored ball, had edged too close to the rim of the lake. His mother, a smoothly rounded woman with crested hair and tapering legs which flashed through the slitted skirt, ran after him, lifted him and carried him, gurgling, to safety.

Dumarest watched them, then looked at the man who sauntered close behind. Not the father or he would have run toward the child. Not even a friend who would have been concerned. And even a stranger would have made some move to avert a possible disaster—unless that stranger had other things on his mind.

"Earl?" Sardia was engrossed with her own problems. "What are we going to do?"

Dumarest remembered their agreement; the partnership she had proposed.

"The stranger," he said. "The one who sold the paintings. A spacer doing a little private trading?"

"A captain," she corrected. "One plying the Rift. He'd gone into a back room and Ahdram called him out to meet me. I think it amused him to introduce us." She added bitterly, "Captain Lon Tuvey chose to be difficult."

"He wouldn't tell you from where he got the paintings?" Dumarest restrained his impatience, the woman would tell it in her own way. "Is that it?"

"Oh, he told me," she admitted. "But it doesn't help. The paintings come from a world in the Rift but he wouldn't tell me the name of the artist. Instead he offered to take me to him and introduce me—for a price." She saw his expression, the shift of his eyes. "No, Earl, not that. He made a point of making it clear he had no use for my body. We wants money. A lot of it."

"For an introduction?"

"That and passage, Earl. A high passage to a world called Ath."

Ath?

Arth?

Earth?

It was incredible, such a coincidence was against all probability, but names could change when affected by time and distance. A shortening, a blurring, a growing carelessness in speech and writing—and one could become the other.

Ath! It was possible, and he couldn't forget the painted moon.

"Earth?" Sardia was staring at him, her eyes widely luminous in the shadowed gloom of the pavilion. "Earl, is something wrong?"

"No." He drew a deep breath. "Are you certain as to the name?"

He saw her nod and fought the sudden blaze of hope within him. Earth, he was certain, could not lie in the Rift. It had to be in a place where stars were few and scattered thin across the sky. The Rift was a swarm of suns burning within a cleft formed by some cosmic disturbance in a cloud of interstellar dust. And yet that very dust would have thinned the stars and created the illusion of remoteness.

Could Ath be the planet for which he had searched for so long?

Could it be Earth?

"Earl!" Sardia was impatient. "We have to decide what to do. We must ride with Tuvey. Even though we know the name of the world we still have to be introduced to the artist so it won't help us to take another ship. And if Tuvey is willing to sell the information to me then he'd sell it to another. He knows the information is valuable now. He could hawk it around—anyone who knows good art will spot the value of those paintings at once and spare no cost to find who produced them."

"He could have lied."

"Yes," she admitted. "But unless we go with him we'll never know. And those paintings he had were genuine. It's a chance we daren't miss. We've got to find the money and arrange the passage. And we have to do it soon. He leaves tomorrow at sunset."

Dumarest glanced at the sky, already the sun was well past the zenith and lowering toward the horizon. Little more than a day to raise how much?

He frowned as she told him. "So much?"

"He's charging high, Earl, but what can we do about it? And we'll need money to arrange a return passage as well as to pay the artist. You have money?"

"A little. And you?"

"My clothes, an open return passage booked to Tonge on the Cheedha Line. I could cancel it and get a refund."

"No." To do that would be to attract possible attention, a fact from which associations could be drawn— never did Dumarest underestimate the power of the Cyclan. "Anything else? You surely didn't give me all of your jewelry? And cash? If you find the artist on Juba you must be able to pay."

"With credit arranged through a commercial house," she explained. "Earl, I'm doing this on my own and I've gone into debt already. Either I find the artist and get his works or I go broke. On Tonge that is serious."

As it was on most commercial worlds with debtors placed under restraint, their labor sold under contract and harsh penalties extracted for non-cooperation. On other worlds, more rigorous, there were no debtors. A man paid for what he got when he got it and if he couldn't pay, then he went without.

"Earl!" She touched his hand and now her voice held pleading. "Please, tell me what to do?"

"Cut your losses and go back home." Advice she didn't want and which he had been stupid to give. His own problems were more serious than hers and to escape the trap closing around him he would need her aid. "But if you want to go ahead then turn everything you've got into money. Your clothes, jewels, everything."

"I have little, Earl. It won't be enough."

"We'll make it grow." Dumarest stared through the lattice-work of the pavilion. At the far edge of the sward a man stood studying the lake, apparently lost in contemplation of the birds which drifted across the surface. "Get moving now. Walk straight ahead and don't look back but when you reach the edge of the grass start running as if you'd seen someone you know."

"Why, Earl?"

"Just do it. Go straight home and sell everything you can. Make sure it's done by sunset. After that wait by your phone."

"And you, Earl?" She shrugged as he didn't answer. "All right, I'll do as you say. But remember—we only have a day to raise the money."

Money—with it the universe was a place of enticing delights, without it a living hell. Money could buy food and comfort, luxury and safety and to get it men were willing to kill and risk being killed, to murder and to die.

"Experience?" The man was plump, sweating, his thin hair plastered over a domed skull. The fabric of his blouse was stained, his belt tightly drawn over a sagging gut. As he spoke he chewed and, at times, spat. "Well?"

"A little," said Dumarest, then quickly corrected himself. "I mean a lot. I'm good and can take care of myself. Just give me a chance, mister, and you won't regret it."

Dowton spat. He'd seen too many like this one before; men with an inflated sense of their own skill and eager to step into the ring and collect the fame and rewards a knife could bring. The game needed them and they could bleed as well as the next, but the crowd was impatient and it was past the time when they would be satisfied with innocents led to the slaughter.

"You've fought in a ring before?"

"Often."

"Where?"

"Back home we had a—" Dumarest shook his head. "On Tonge," he said. "And on Embirha. I've fought often and I'm good." His laugh was strained. "I'm alive to prove it."

Dowton said, "Strip and let's take a look."

He sucked in his breath as he saw the naked torso, the thin lines of old scars which laced the flesh. At least this one would look good and it would do no harm to face the champ with someone who, at least, must have learned how to dodge.

"Here!" Knives lay on a table, murderous ten-inch blades. Picking up one he threw it, frowned as Dumarest missed the catch. "Slow, eh?"

"I speed up when warm." Dumarest hefted the blade with deliberate awkwardness, accentuating the picture he had drawn, that of a hopeful, not totally inexperienced but of no real danger to any fighter who knew his trade. He said earnestly, "I can put on a show and I need the money."

"It's to the death—you realize that?"

"Mister, if I don't get some money soon I'll be dead anyway. What's the fee?" He blinked. "A hundred? That all?"

"Back it on yourself and you could collect five." A safe bet, this fool would never live to collect. Dowton added, "If you're smart you'll take my advice. Yhma is getting past it. Once he's down you'll be the new champ. Well?"

"I'll take it," said Dumarest. "Five hundred when I win. Right? When do I fight?"

"Later. You'll be called. Just sit around and wait."

Wait as the roar from the seats surrounding the ring grew louder as contenders met and fought to leave blood and life in the arena. Savage, vicious combats which played to the blood lust of those watching; the decadents and degenerates who emerged like nocturnal vermin to enter the Maze at night.

A sound as familiar to Dumarest as was the smell, the compound of oil and sweat, of blood and antiseptics, the whole dominated by the acrid taint of fear.

He sat on a bench he'd found in a dressing room, leaning back against the wall, eyes half-closed as he reviewed recent events. The field was sealed as he'd suspected, men at the gates and on patrol, all entering checked and interrogated. On a more primitive world there would have been ways to dodge the guards but here on Juba the fence was ninety feet high, set with tiers of lights, fitted with alarms and surrounded by a fifty-foot ditch edged with metal spikes.

Even so, with enough money something could have been arranged given time, but he had no money and time was running out.

The trap he was in was set to close.

And, when it did, he would be a prisoner of the Cyclan.

Dumarest had no illusions as to what would happen then. He would be probed, interrogated, questioned with a penetrating skill, the very cells of his brain torn

INCIDENT ON ATH

apart so as to win his secret. And then, when that was done, he would be disposed of as so much rubbish.

"You all right?" A man stared through the open door. He was old, grinning, the scar on his cheek a livid weal. "Scared? Want a nip to warm you up?"

Dumarest took the proffered bottle, lifted it to his lips, his throat working as he pretended to drink. If the man was attached to Yhma the stuff would be spiked with some insidious drug—an elementary precaution.

"Good, eh?" The grin widened. "Take some more if you want. It'll give you an edge. Say, if you've got some money I could lay it for you. Odds are four to one."

Dumarest shook his head. Sardia held his money and should now be in the stands. When the time was ripe she would place her bets, using everything they had between them, risking poverty on his skill.

Risking poverty as he was risking his life.

He wondered what she would do if he were to die.

It would come one day and that day could be now. A slip, a momentary inattention, an accident and he could fall with his guts slashed open, the intestines spilling like a coil of greasy rope, blood falling to drench his thighs and feet as eternal darkness closed around him. A small thing could do it. A trifle—and yet it would cost him the universe of his awareness.

"You ready?" A youngster this time, a boy with wide eyes bright with hero worship. "Greg told me to warn you. He's waiting at the entry—say, you ever fought before?"

"I've got by."

"Yhma's put down two already. The first was for third blood and he drew it out; a cut to the left arm, another on the flank then finish!" The boy made an expressive gesture. "He slid the blade right into the guts, a twist and it was done. Blood everywhere. The crowd loved it."

And a man had died without need.

"The other?"

"He lasted longer," admitted the boy. "But only because he was scared. He just kept backing and dodging until the champ had enough. Then he moved in, dropped to one knee, a slash and he'd hamstrung the challenger. That was first blood."

"Then what? He take out the eyes?"

"No." The boy missed the irony. "Nothing like that. He was gentle. A couple of cuts, one across the inside of each elbow and that was all."

Gentle! A man crippled in one leg, both arms rendered useless from severed tendons, and all without need. A touch would have been enough. The merest sight of blood would have determined the victor.

"A nice man," said Dumarest. "I bet you've learned a lot watching him. What's his favorite trick?"

For a moment he thought the boy would answer then a veil dropped over the shining eyes. "You're fighting to the death, right?"

"That's right."

"Watch Yhma's left hand. Sometimes he crosses the blade and when he does he moves in with a feint from the right."

Lies, the boy would not sell out his hero, but even so the trick could work if the situation were right.

"His left hand, eh?" Dumarest looked thoughtful. "Thanks. I'll give you ten when I collect."

"Make it a score." The boy turned as someone yelled. "That's Greg. Hurry now, you're on."

The ring was a square a dozen feet on a side; too small for easy maneuver and not large enough for any fighter to use speed to gain distance and so extend the action. A bad ring and an ugly crowd, one which yelled as Dumarest climbed on the platform, their voices joining in an incoherent yammer. But if he couldn't make out the words he knew their meaning. Blood! Blood! Blood and death! Wounds and pain!

INCIDENT ON ATH

The roar of the beast which showed itself in avid eyes and faces more animal than human.

Yhma took his time and, waiting, Dumarest looked around. Suspended over the ring, lights threw down a searing cone of brilliance which left the tiers of seats in relative gloom. Only those close to the ringside were clearly visible, their occupants all expensively dressed, both men and women heavily jeweled. A matron with raddled cheeks stared at him and made a lewd comment to a man who tittered and passed on the snippet to a languid girl who yawned and slowly drew her nails over his cheek.

Degenerates and typical of those who had paid high prices for their seats. Higher in the tiers would be others, less wealthy but just as depraved, and Sardia should be among them.

Dumarest turned, staring, narrowing his eyes against the glare of the overhead lights. He couldn't spot her but the failure meant little. All aside from those in the first few rows were little more than formless blurs in the shrouding gloom. But if the plan was to work she must be watching and, if it was to work well, she had to have been there from the beginning.

The clash of a gong and the champion appeared.

Yhma was tall, lithe, built with a feline grace, arms long, knotted with cords of writhing muscle, traced with the ropes of veins. He had legs to match and his torso, above the narrow waist, was a sculptor's dream. A barrel, rigid with clearly delineated muscle, swelling to the massive shoulders which in turn supported the surprisingly slender neck. A man as dark as seasoned teak, glistening with oil, his hair a cropped fuzz, the blade in his hand an icicle of destruction. His face was that of a brooding idol, the nostrils flared, the bridge hooked, the mouth soft with a deceptive pout.

A veteran as the scars signified, thin cicatrices of healed tissue which traced a web over the oiled hide. The penalty paid for hard-won tuition and his eyes widened as he saw the matching lines which Dumarest displayed.

"A change, my friend. You, I see, are far from a witless hunk of meat. We shall have fun, I think."

A blade slashing tendons, one slipping into the stomach, the edge used to cripple and maim—fun?

"You have nothing to say to me?" Light splintered as Yhma turned his blade. "No word of grace to give a man you would like to kill? How would you like to do it, my friend? A clean thrust into the heart? One into the spleen? A single blow which could make your fortune. You see those women in the front rows? Kill me and each of them will fall into your arms. And the men—" His smile widened. "Think of it, friend. A single thrust and all could be yours."

And, if he concentrated on making that thrust, he would be dead.

Dumarest knew it as he knew the talk was to distract and so to weaken. As yet the combat hadn't begun but no true fighter waited for the gong. If the knife couldn't be used then words also had an edge. As the ripple of muscle in the near-naked body could spell a message. As the stance could induce despair.

Dumarest backed until he felt the rope press against his back. Like Yhma he wore brief shorts and nothing else aside from the oil which numbed the flesh a little and which made it almost impossible for an opponent to retain a grip. Leaning back he studied the man who intended to kill him.

A sadist—that he had learned from the boy. A skilled fighter—that he had learned from the way the man stood and moved and kept himself in balance. A dangerous one—that was obvious from his victories. But how dangerous?

He straightened to the sound of the gong. When next it clashed combat would begin and a second's delay in getting ready could mean giving the other a chance. He watched the position of Yhma's feet, the ripple of muscle in calves and thighs. A man poised to leap in any direction, one set to twist and turn, to create a barrier of edged and pointed steel between himself and the one who opposed him. And smooth.

Dumarest lifted his eyes, checking minor points, assessing, noting the feline grace.

Smooth and quick and neatly precise. The knife was held in the usual sword fashion, thumb to the blade, the point slightly lifted. A normal grasp, but in Yhma's hand it looked like a scalpel in a surgeon's grip. Dumarest hefted his own weapon, a twin of the other. It was too long for his liking, lacking the fine balance needed for an accurate throw. But, in this ring, there would be no need of that.

"You sweat," said Yhma softly. "You betray your fear but, my friend, have no fear. We are to fight to the death but it need not come to that. A few exchanges, a little blood, a wound and you fall to lie still and so to live and maybe fight again. An arrangement, you understand? Life, my friend. Life. There is no need for you to die."

The promise offered, the lie which only a fool would believe. A fool or a man desperate to live no matter what the cost. Bait offered to a man who, mentally, was already beaten. A bribe to succumb to the kiss of his blade.

How many had died when thinking they would live?

"You mean that?" asked Dumarest. Like the other he kept his voice down. "You mean you'd give me a chance?"

"To live? Yes, my friend." Teeth flashed white as Yhma smiled. We will play a little first, you understand. A sop to the crowd. Some blood from minor wounds—you have my word they will be that. Then, when the time is right, I'll give the word. We meet, strike, you miss and I'll give you a wound. You fall and that will be it. You agree?"

"Yes."

"Good." The smile widened. "You are wise."

Wise in the ways of the ring and a liar when it came to the promise, but the lie can gain an advantage and all was fair when life was at stake.

A lesson Dumarest had learned when a novice. He had believed a man and had almost died because of it, only his speed saving him from a blow which would have gutted a normal man. The speed which would have to save him now.

He was moving before the clash of the gong had died, not toward Yhma but to one side, turning as the other lunged, steel clashing as the blades touched, rasping as they slid one over the other, ringing as they parted. An exchange which won a gasp from the crowd.

"Yhma get him!" A woman screamed the command. "A hundred if you hit him first!"

"Two hundred if you spike an eye!"

"Fifty if you make him hop!"

Offers born of the side bets and invitations to cruelty. Dumarest ignored them as he concentrated on his opponent. Yhma shifted like a cat, poised on the balls of his feet, light flashing from the knife, to vanish, to appear as the blade lanced forward, to cut, to miss and cut again.

To fetch a tide of red oozing from Dumarest's arm.

"A hit! First blood to Yhma!" The woman's scream echoed from the upper tiers. "Shout for the champion!"

Sardia? It could have been anyone. The voice had been disguised by echoes and passion. Dumarest backed, feeling the sting of the cut. A shallow wound which looked far worse than it really was. One he had invited and deliberately taken in order to increase the odds against him.

But Yhma looked puzzled and Dumarest knew why. The man hadn't intended to hit. His blade should have missed by a fraction and would have had not Dumarest moved into its path. A calculated maneuver—a wound chosen was better than one taken by chance.

Yet an ordinary fighter wouldn't have worried about it, imagining himself to be better than he'd thought. The victory would have been enough. Winning a hit would have made him a little more confident. A little less careful.

But Yhma?

Dumarest tensed as the man came in, twisting, blocking, the knives clashing as they touched to part to touch again in a metallic music which held the prelude to a dirge. A flurry of attack, parry, thrust and riposte, engage and counter-engage. Air whined as edges slicked toward flesh, to miss, to sweep back in protective glitters. Between them the naked steel flashed like mirrors and rang like hostile bells.

Yhma was fast. Faster than any normal man. Faster even than himself.

Looking at him Dumarest saw death.

Chapter Five

First it had been vile, bearable only because of the job which had to be done, then, oddly and shamefully, interest had grown and with it an appreciation of the skills involved and now something else had been added, an emotion which threatened to overwhelm her with an intoxicating intensity.

The euphoria of blood! Where had she heard that? *The aphrodisiac of pain!*

Someone else's blood, of course, and another's pain, but the euphoria was real and also the sexual stimulation. She felt it, recognized the fever in her blood, the heat suffusing her loins. Touching her breasts she found the nipples hard, prominent against the thin fabric of her gown. If Dumarest had been at her side she would have clutched him with thoughtless abandon as other women clutched at their men.

Dumarest was not beside her but in the ring below fighting for the money they needed.

Fighting for his life.

"A hit!" The yell rose from the lower tiers. "Third blood!"

Two wounds to add to the first and more blood to dapple the hard whiteness of his skin. And, as yet, Yhma was unmarked. A feral machine of corded muscle which moved like a flickering illusion. Fast. So very fast. Too fast, perhaps, and if Dumarest should die?

"Seven to one on the champion!" yelled a gambler. "One gets you seven if Dumarest wins!"

"A fool's bet," snapped a man. "I'll take seven hundred on Yhma."

And would win a hundred if the champion should win. Easy money and certain from the look of it. And yet. . . .

Sardia trembled in indecision. To risk everything on what seemed to be a lost hope or to do as Dumarest had ordered despite appearances? To gamble on an apparent certainty or to remain loyal?

But if Dumarest should fall?

"Seven to one," yelled the gambler. Then, as the crowd roared as Dumarest stumbled, missing the thrust of Yhma's blade by a seeming miracle, "Eight! Eight to one! Who wants to take it?"

"I do!"

The words were out, the decision made, all she had was now riding on the blood-stained figure in the ring. With others she rose to her feet as again Dumarest stumbled, to regain his balance with an effort, to move, knife flashing, to dodge and turn, to throw a quick glance toward where she stood.

"Earl!" Her voice was a cry which cut through the noise with pulsing clarity. "Win, Earl! Win!"

He hadn't seen her, of that she was certain, but he might have heard her. To be sure she shouted again.

"Win, Earl! Win!"

A cry taken up by others swaying to the whim of the moment. One which spread as ripples from a stone thrown into water. A roar of encouragement from those who, illogically, hastened to bet on a forlorn cause.

The madness of the arena and its attraction.

It gripped her as it gripped others, accentuating her physical reaction so that she felt herself being lifted high into vibrating life. Colors became sharper, the air clearer, senses more acute. As if it had been a potent drug, she responded to the atmosphere, the sight of blood, the spectacle of men fighting to kill.

"Win, Earl! Win!"

Cut and stab and send your knife deep into living flesh. Show us his blood. Give us his pain. Let us see you kill and let us watch him die.

Vileness!

And yet still she could not look away.

The ring was a stage and the crowd a muted orchestra, the pulse of drums echoing from the roof above as, centered in the spotlights, the dancers weaved in an elaborate saraband. Outrousky had composed such a ballet and she had danced in it playing the part of the woman for whom men had fought. She remembered the slow commencement, the maintained tempo, the sudden, frightening burst of frenzied activity, the slow, solemn movements of the finale. Now she moved to the rhythm again, body rippling beneath her gown, feeling the rising of tension as, below her, men moved in the most significant dance ever created.

One which only a single person would survive.

"Bastard!" Yhma was gripped by the rage of fear. "You bastard!"

Dumarest smiled.

An act; he had no cause for amusement, but it helped to increase Yhma's anger and a fighter blinded with temper was that much less a threat. And the main cause for his anger: the one who had seemed an easy victim had lied, had made him appear a fool, had survived too long despite his quickness. And, worse, had a speed of his own.

A darting, gliding, flashing quickness which had extended the bout and made him, finally, begin to have fears for his own safety.

Dumarest was wounded, but the second cut on the thigh was minor as was the first. Only the third, a deep gash on the side, would weaken with a steady loss of blood. A fact Dumarest knew as well as the man he faced.

Yhma was clever, using his blade as a fighter should, cutting to sever tendons, open veins, slashing at muscles. Crippling with an accumulation of wounds before delivering the final blow. A spectacle which pleased the crowd and satisfied his sadistic nature. Dumarest too used the edge but had been forced to extend the combat, to miss when he could have hit, to take chances at first and then, when recognizing his danger, to nurse his strength.

He had not wanted the wounds received after the first. He had not wanted the continual play of blades and ceaseless movements—for the plan made with Sardia to work, time was needed to instill his inadequacy in the crowd. The original plan abandoned when he realized his opponent's full potential.

Now the need wasn't for high odds but simply to stay alive.

"Bastard!" said Yhma again. "You stinking, dirty bastard!"

An old trick and Dumarest wondered why the man had tried it. Surely he must know by now that taunts would serve no purpose? Better he should wait, conserve his breath, let his superior conditioning win him the greater edge. An edge Dumarest was doing his best to eliminate.

Yhma was skilled, fast, a conditioned fighter in the peak of training. Younger, fitter and with a speed to match Dumarest's own, he should have won without trouble. But that very speed now told against him. Too often it had gained him victory without the added ingredient of skill; the skill Dumarest had hard-won over the years.

Yhma was an animal, slowing a little now, baffled by his failure to drive home his blade, angry and letting anger affect his judgment. Steel rang as the knives met, rang again, thin, clear notes which rose above the tense hush which gripped the crowd. No one was shouting now. Standing, eyes focused on the brilliance of the ring, every man and woman was conscious of the extra dimension the struggle had taken.

Muscle and hate matched against muscle and brain.

A drama of life and death which filled the place as would the tension generated by an electrical storm.

"Now!" gasped a woman in the front row. "Now!"

A flurry of blades, a feint, a parry, a feint followed by a disengage and then another feint, light flashing from honed steel, winking, catching the eye.

And, suddenly, Dumarest had the edge.

He knew it, could feel it and was acting even as the knowledge registered. Again his blade flashed, moved, holding Yhma's eyes, distracting his attention as his free hand scraped a palmful of blood from his oozing wound. Blood which he flung into the champion's eyes as he dropped, reaching out, edged steel hitting, biting, dragging deep as he drew it back across the rear of the naked knee.

He rolled as the crowd roared, rising to his feet to block a downward cut, moving again to one side, moving again as Yhma spun and staggered as his hamstrung leg yielded beneath his weight.

"You—!"

Rage and fear left him open and his own inclinations had betrayed him. In such a case after giving such a wound he would have taken time to gloat, to play to the crowd, to anticipate the next hit and to enjoy the other's terror and pain.

The weakness of a skilled amateur as was the curse he had tried to utter. An obscenity which died as Dumarest closed the space between them, flashing splinters darting from the blade in his hand. The knife which slashed at the tendons on Yhma's wrist. The steel which cut again as the blade fell from the injured hand.

To touch the side of the throat, to open the skin, the fat, the flesh beneath. To reach the throbbing carotid

INCIDENT ON ATH 67

artery and to release the champion's life in a jetting fountain of smoking blood.

The officer at the gate was tall, young, darkly handsome and with an appreciative eye for feminine beauty. He watched as the cab drew to a halt, stooping to look inside, smiling at the woman the passenger compartment contained.

"Madam?"

Sardia del Naeem said, "I've passage booked on the *Sivas*. Captain Lon Tuvey. May I pass through?"

Regretfully the officer shook his head. "Not in that vehicle, I'm afraid. You'll have to step out and be checked. You have luggage?"

"Yes." She gestured at the small suitcase beside her. "Do you mean I'll have to walk to the vessel?"

"We can supply a jitney. Is this all the luggage you have?"

"Of course not. There is more in the trunk."

The cab had a large carrying capacity now almost wholly utilized by the long, squared cabin trunk it contained, the two large suitcases. The officer pursed his lips as he looked at them. The woman, obviously, was not the male fugitive whom he had been ordered to watch for and detain if found and he knew females too well to be deluded by a man wearing their garb. Perhaps, just to make certain, he should order her to be searched? Then, as she smiled at him and casually moved so as to throw into prominence the swell of her breasts and the rounded curves of hips and buttocks, he decided against it.

But the luggage was a different matter.

"The *Sivas*, you say?"

"Yes. Captain Lon Tuvey. You know him? I found him a most charming man but a little on the eccentric side if you know what I mean. He simply refused to tell me just when he was leaving. I had to be on board at sunset, he said, but when is that? After the sun has lowered beneath the horizon or when it grows dark or what?" Alarm edged her voice, making it shrill, unmistakably feminine. "The ship is still here? I'm not too late?"

"No," he said and smiled to reassure her. "You're in good time."

"And the jitney will take me and my luggage out to the vessel?"

A nervous type, he decided, and one not accustomed to traveling alone. No woman with her face and figure need do that; always there would be someone willing to foot the bills and take care of the details. A quarrel with some lover, perhaps? If so the man had been a fool to allow her to escape.

He signaled to the jitney and looked again at the luggage as it drew to a halt beside the cab. The small suitcase stood beside the woman where she had placed it on leaving the vehicle. The cabin trunk and the two large suitcases remained to be unloaded.

"Rud!"

The driver of the jitney joined him as the officer reached for the cabin trunk. He grunted as he grabbed a handle and strained.

"Heavy!" The driver spat on his hands. "Together now!"

A heave and it was done, the box set on the loading bed of the jitney. Turning, the officer saw Sardia, one of the large suitcases at her feet. She was straining at the other and looked appealingly at him.

"Could you? Please!"

It lifted in his grip and he swung it and set it down beside the box. As he straightened, Sardia set the other beside it, turning away, stooping to reach for the small case which remained.

The driver said, "What about the box, sir?"

A reminder, but the officer hadn't forgotten. It was large enough to hold a man and heavy enough to arouse suspicion. The woman, despite her attraction, could be involved and, if the box did hold the wanted man, the reward would be high.

"The box, madam," he said. "Please open it."

"Must I?" Her eyes betrayed her reluctance. "I mean, is it normal? I've often traveled before and I've never yet been searched like this. Have you the right to demand such a thing?"

"I've the right." And the power too if he wanted to exercise it. Without further argument he tested the lid and found it locked. "The key if you please." Her hand shook a little as she gave it to him. "Thank you."

Lifting the lid he saw a cloth and, throwing it to one side, stared blankly at what the box contained.

"I'm sorry," she said. "I didn't think I was doing anything wrong. I was only trying to help a friend."

"Figures!" Rud, the driver, snorted his disappointment. "A mess of carvings!"

"Works of art," explained Sardia. "That's my business. I deal in works of art, buying, selling, trading when I have to. I've found the most interesting pieces and I'm sure the museum back home will be glad to put them on display with a little card crediting them to me. A way of advertising you understand. The curator and I have an understanding." Hesitating, she added, "There's no law against my having them, is there? I mean, on some worlds you have to get permission to export rare and valuable items. That's why I didn't want to open the box. I mean, that is—well, I'm sorry."

She made a small gesture with her hands and stood, blushing, a woman confessing her guilt.

"Junk!" muttered the driver. "A lot of rubbish!"

"Get to your seat." The man was right but who was he to deflate the woman's ego? Smiling, the officer said, "You've nothing to worry about, madam. Juba has no prohibition on the export of such items." Locking the box he handed her the keys and then, on impulse, said, "But I'd like to take a look into one of your cases."

"Which?" Her hand rested on the one she had lifted. "This?"

"The other one." She had made hard work of it though he had lifted it without strain. Then the illogic of it struck him as a siren echoed over the field. The case, though large, was still too small to contain a man and certainly didn't have the weight. "Never mind. That siren was from the *Sivas*. Take her over to the ship, Rud. Have a pleasant journey, madam."

Her smile answered his salute. At the vessel the handler grunted at the weight of the box then heaved it on the loading ramp. One of the suitcases followed and he caught Sardia as, after setting down the other, she staggered.

"You all right, my lady?"

"Yes. They will stay in the hold?"

"Until we lift and then I'll get them to your cabin if you want." The handler glanced at the sky. "Ten minutes and we'll be on our way."

Ten minutes—she had timed it well. And another thirty before the handler came puffing to the door of her cabin, his eyes reproachful as he heaved at the suitcases. Locking the door behind him she busied herself with her keys. The lid of one of the cases lifted.

Dumarest was huddled inside.

He was wasted, gaunt, fat and watery tissue burned away during the time he had waited in the woman's apartment after the fight. Hours spent beneath the influence of slow-time, the drug which had increased his metabolism and turned ordinary hours into subjective days. Time for his wounds to heal. Time for his weight and bulk to diminish—but even so it had been close.

He was naked, the weight of his clothing, boots and knife carried in the other suitcase, the garments mixed with others of a similar nature which were hers. Things bought as the carvings had been to aid the deception.

"Earl!" Gently she eased him from the cramped confines. "Earl?"

He gasped with the pain of returning circulation. He had been in the case little more than an hour but it had seemed an eternity and, to fit into it at all, muscles had to be strained and joints distorted so as to take advantage of every scrap of room.

A trick learned when he'd worked in a carnival from a girl who had been kind. She'd been able to cram her body into a cube little more than a foot on a side and had taken pleasure in teaching him how the body could be bent, turned, the head lowered, the legs folded, the arms wrapped so as to form a compact bundle.

"Earl?"

"I'm all right." He straightened, conscious of her anxiety, breath hissing from between his teeth as he massaged various points. "How long?"

"We left almost an hour ago. You're safe now."

Safe from what she didn't know and hadn't asked. It had been a matter of mutual need. He had won the money and she'd helped him elude the trap. A gamble on her loyalty and the strength gained in the execution of her art. One almost lost when, at the ramp, that strength had almost failed her.

Now she closed the distance between them, touching his body, her fingers tracing the points of recent wounds. Scars now faded and blending with the rest.

But he was thin! So thin!

Gently he moved away from her touch and, guessing his need, she opened the other case and produced his clothing. Dressed he looked more like his normal self but his face held the taut hardness of a skull.

"Earl, you need food."

"Later," said Dumarest. "First we must see the captain."

He joined them where they waited in the salon, a short man with broad shoulders and a face seamed and lined like a dried fruit. His eyes were splinters of amber glass set beneath bushy brows. His hair was a grizzled cap hugging a peaked skull. His uniform was of fine material, bright with carefully tended insignia. On his left shoulder rode a thing from a nightmare.

A creature like a crab, spined, claws serrated with vicious indentations, an extension like a segmented tail over the rounded shoulders, smaller appendages like miniature hands which served to carry food to the snapping mandibles. The eyes were like jewels set on hornlike promontories.

Captain Lon Tuvey was an unusual man.

"So." He paused in the doorway looking at Sardia then at Dumarest who had helped himself to a cup of basic. "It appears we have a stowaway."

"A passenger," corrected the woman. "Earl is a passenger."

"Earl?" His eyes narrowed as she gave the rest of the name. "Earl Dumarest. No such person is listed on my records. No such person was seen to board the *Sivas*. No such person has the right to be on my ship." His voice was a drone of mechanical precision. "As far as I'm concerned he is nothing but a stowaway. Need I tell you the penalty for riding a vessel without permission?"

"I know the penalty," said Dumarest. "But you won't have to evict me. I can pay."

"And if I refuse to carry you?" The amber eyes flickered as Dumarest set down the cup. "You recognize my authority?"

"Not if it means going meekly through a port."

"No," said Tuvey. "I didn't think you would. Well, we have no cause to argue, if you have money all is well." He glanced at the woman. "You travel together? As I thought. The price will be double that arranged."

Dumarest said coldly, "I'm not interested in meeting an artist."

"Then you shouldn't be on my ship." Lifting a hand Tuvey drummed his fingernails on the carapace of his pet. "And if you want to argue the matter both the steward and the handler are, at this moment, covering you with lasers."

And somewhere would be the navigator and the engineer with, perhaps, an assistant or two.

"No," said Dumarest. "I don't want to argue."

"A wise man and your wisdom has bought you a bonus. I shall not return to Juba to discover if you are the man the guards are looking for. The cost and inconvenience wouldn't cover the reward—not when you consider the lost passage money." Again his fingers made small drumming sounds as they impacted the shell. Watching, Dumarest saw the segmented tail lift and the spined legs stiffen as if the creature enjoyed the tapping. "It does." Tuvey had guessed the curiosity. Borol appreciates the rhythm. I call him that because he reminds me of an officer I once knew. He fell into a vat of petrifying liquids and he, too, had a hard shell."

Dumarest said dryly, "But not for long."

"No." Tuvey set down the creature which scuttled into a corner to turn and freeze and watch with unblinking eyes. "You've been riding Low?"

"Yes." A lie but it would serve.

"And so need building up. Take all the basic you need—it is included in the price." As would be the quick-time they would be given later, the magic of the drug slowing down metabolism as slow-time quickened it. A convenience which shortened the tedium of long journeys. "How did you get aboard?"

"In the trunk." Dumarest met the shrewd amber of the eyes. If Tuvey thought he was lying he gave no sign. "How long will it take us to reach Ath?"

"Does it matter?" The captain smiled as he glanced at Sardia. "With such a companion what importance has time? Rest, eat, relax and enjoy yourselves. How many have such an opportunity?"

A chance to do as he suggested—but even with normal hours shrunken to apparent seconds, time needed filling. Talk did it, whispers in the darkness as they lay close, memories recounted as they sat in gentle illumination with the pleasure of wine adding to their intimacy.

Sardia spoke of her youth, of the harsh discipline of the Corps Mantage, of artists she had known and now would never see again.

"Amil was the best, Earl. A dancer infused with the flame of genius. A man dedicated to the art. When he was on stage not a whisper could be heard from the audience. On Chrachery, when a man coughed, he was almost killed for what the others chose to regard as an insult. And, when he finally died, the queue to see him lying in state stretched for miles. It took days for them all to pay their last homage and each day fresh blooms are placed on his monument."

"You knew him?"

"He died in my arms." She fell silent, brooding, and he knew better than to break into her mood. Instead he sipped more basic; the fluid sickly with glucose, laced with vitamins, thick with protein. A cupful was the normal ration for a day.

Thoughtfully he studied the woman.

Amil had died in her arms and the man had been the hero of a world if what she said was true. Which meant that she, herself, must have achieved a high degree of fame. And, while she lacked the boyishness of a young girl, she was far from old.

"Even so I'm too old," she said when he put the question. "Nothing is more pathetic than a dancer who clings too long to a fading reputation. I could have used drugs but such things are crutches and being at the top makes you a target for those eager to climb. Then Amil died and Verecunda hurt herself and I decided it was time to make a graceful exit and take up something else." She shook her head, dismissing ghosts. "And you, Earl? What about you?"

"I travel."

"And?" She shook him, her hand warm against his

bare shoulder. They had loved and were resting and it was a time for reminiscences. "Your childhood, what about that? And what made you leave home?"

She frowned as he told her, knowing he was skipping, leaving much unsaid and conscious of the gaps. A bleak and harsh childhood, a time of savage necessity with hunger as a constant companion. The need which had set him wandering to find a ship on which he had stowed away. A captain who had been more than kind.

"He could have evicted me," said Dumarest. "Instead, he let me work my passage and took care of me as best he could."

A surrogate father who had died to leave the youngster to wander alone. Moving ever deeper into the heart of the galaxy where worlds were close and ships plentiful. To regions where even the name of Earth had been forgotten.

"And now you want to find it," she said. "You want to get back home. But, Earl, are you sure?"

"About the name?" He had recognized her tone. "I'm sure."

"A world of legend," she murmured. "A myth—even the name makes it unreal. Earth! Why not call it dirt or soil or sand? And you have been searching for it how long?"

Too long, riding High when he could and Low when he couldn't; locked in a casket designed for the transportation of beasts, doped, frozen, ninety percent dead and risking the fifteen percent death rate for the sake of cheap transportation. A bad way to ride, one which robbed the body of fat and excess tissue—no wonder Tuvey had jumped to that conclusion.

"Earl!" Her hand caressed his naked flesh. Already he was filling out, the basic he took together with added ingestors replacing the starved tissues. "Such a hard life."

Had there been no comfort in it at all? No beauty?

Beauty enough, she decided; the vistas of new

worlds, the panorama of space itself, the planetary spectacles which tourists paid highly to see. And there would have been comfort in the form of women if nothing else. His masculinity would have attracted them as a flame attracted moths and they would have flocked to him after his fight in the ring.

She remembered again how he had looked when facing Yhma, the hard savagery of his face, the cruel mouth, the deathly eyes. Eyes matched by the cold flicker of naked steel, the body a symphony of quick and graceful movement. And then the bursting effort of the finale when, as graceful as a dancer, he had cut and cut again to disarm and release the jetting fountain of a human life. A gushing stream which had lifted the crowd to its feet screaming approbation.

A screaming in which she had joined as her body had trembled and jerked to the fury of orgasmic release.

Chapter Six

They landed at sunset when the sky was a vista of entrancing color; swaths of red and orange, blue and umber, green, yellow, azure tinted with shimmers of gold, somber browns illuminated with flecks of puffy whiteness. A splendor due to airborne dusts and aerial microorganisms which caught and reflected the rays of the dying orb.

The town beyond the field matched the beauty of the sky.

Broad terraces surrounded a lake of flowered water, a central fountain casting a perpetual rain. Others set at the edges giving birth to a rainbowed mist. On the terraces, set like jewels on a string, houses merged with greenery and the gentle mask of trees. Spired, turreted, some with cathedral-like soaring arches, others a compact blend of curve and line having the strength and functional beauty of a clenched fist. A multitude of architectural styles married into a common harmony.

"Ath," said Tuvey. His hand lifted to rap the shell of the pet riding his shoulder. "You like it?"

"It's lovely!" Sardia clutched Dumarest's arm. "So clean! So neat! So much like a . . . a . . ."

A child's toy. Dumarest fitted the words to the incompleted sentence as he stood looking at the city. It was too neat, too precise. A normal, living city was never that. It held noise and bustle and a certain untidiness and always a little dirt. A place in which people moved and worked and had their being. This was more like a calculated design; one planned down to the last detail and all offensive or obtrusive intrusions carefully removed. A construct made by detached planners who cared more for the esthetic appearance than for the comfort of those who had to reside in it.

And yet even that was not wholly true.

"It's like a house," whispered Sardia. "One over which generations have labored so as to get it just right. Or a room furnished and decorated to the exact liking of its owner. It's perfect, Earl. Perfect!"

As a cut and faceted gem, a carving, a mosaic. A thing complete and set for all to admire. An artistic achievement as a single house could be, a single room. But no living city could ever be that.

"Listen," he said and then, as Sardia, obeying, frowned, he added, "no children. You can't hear any children."

There were green spaces and walks and little copses and shelters which childish imagination could turn into jungles and forests and eerie castles. Places which were ripe for mental conversion into haunts of mystery—and yet no shrill voices rose above the susurration of the fountains and nowhere on the terraces could children be seen.

Tuvey shrugged as Sardia questioned him as to their absence.

"Don't ask me. I land, I trade, I leave and what goes on behind city walls is none of my concern. You paid for passage and you got it. The journey is all your money bought."

A long journey, too long in the Rift where worlds were close and Dumarest suspected the man of deliberate detours so as to lenghten the time. To make sure he wasn't being followed? Traders such as the captain often hugged the secret of profitable ports to themselves.

He said dryly, "A correction, Captain. We bought a little more than passage."

"An introduction also, I haven't forgotten." Tuvey's fingers rasped over the carapace of his pet. "But that was for the woman. You, Earl, will find other guesting."

"Guesting?"

"You'll see." The captain gestured toward the city. "Here they come."

They were like fireflies, or, no, like clowns, but that was wrong also and Dumarest blinked to clear his mind and eyes of first impressions. Perspective had done it and the neat array of bizarre dwellings. Their owners were the same. Like the buildings, they verged on the edge of fantasy and yet nothing about them was other than decorative or functional. Clothing, oddly cut, oddly draped, still served a purpose. Colors, brilliantly applied, still held a form of logical usage. Lips tinted ochre were still lips clearly delineated. Hair rippling with shimmering hues was still hair clean and adorning rather than disguising the faces beneath.

"The stage," said Sardia blankly. "They look as if they're all taking part in a play of some kind. A fantasy such as Synthe's *Transpadane*. I danced in it when young. Earl, this is wonderful!"

For her, yes, because for her it was normal, the life she had once known and had perhaps known better than the later, wasting years. The world of make-believe of which she had been a part when everything was other than what it seemed and all was possible at the touch of imagination's wand. But his universe was of harsher fabric and in it the strange was also the potentially dangerous, and things which were not genuine were always worse than what they appeared.

"Sardia!"

He was too late, already she had gone, running to meet the brilliant cluster coming to greet the new arrivals.

At his side Tuvey said, "Let her go. Later I'll see she

meets her artist." Then, oddly, he added, "I wonder what you'll fetch?"

Fetch? A question quickly answered as a dozen bright figures crowded around. One, dressed in dull green slashed with flaming scarlet, feathers on rump and ankles, a crest riding high on his skull, stamped close. With him came the tintinnabulation of tiny bells.

"Captain! Again you honor us. One thousand for the Captain!"

"And a half!" A woman, smooth flesh gleaming naked beneath the slashed vents in her gown, her hair silvered, her lips and nails colored to match, her eyes the color of minted gold, topped the bid.

"Two!" The third voice was deeper, older. "You had him the last time, Myrna."

"True." The silvered woman shrugged. "Then two for the other."

"Three!"

"Five!"

"And a half!"

"It's too much! And it's my turn. "Six!"

Dumarest frowned as he listened, seeing Tuvey smile, the person who had won him now standing close to his side. An older woman with a lined face deliberately accentuated so as to present the appearance of a crone. One belied by the firm curvature of her body.

"Is this a game, Captain?"

"No game, Earl, but no harm in it either. A local custom and it's best to play along. There are no taverns here and no hotels. To find accommodation you have to be a guest and this is the guesting. You stay with the one who wins you. Stay long enough and you could be passed on. Entertain well enough and you could gain the original bidder a profit."

A custom rooted in boredom but one which the residents took seriously. The voices rose higher, became sharper, the bids joined now with argument.

"Ten and I should have him. Always I have to wait."

INCIDENT ON ATH

"Eleven and stop crying, Verrania. Be nice to me and, maybe, I'll let you talk to him."

"Bitch!"

"Cow!"

"You filthy harlot! I'll teach you a lesson in good manners!"

A flurry quickly smoothed, the two women meeting to be parted with no more damage than a ripped garment. Dumarest looked up and away from the crowd, looking at the rim of a terrace, seeing a silent, watchful figure standing in the shadows of a flowering tree. One different from those who stood before him in both manner and dress. A woman with close-cropped hair of reddish gold, a square, determined face, a figure which even beneath the dark pants and blouse she wore he could tell was firm and muscular. A moment and then she was gone and a new voice rose amid the others.

"Fifteen! I bid fifteen."

"Ursula—"

"And I'll take it as a personal insult if any should bid against me." Her voice held the sweet venom of honeyed poison. "Myrna? No, I thought not. Glissa? You, too, are wise. "Cheryl?" A moment as the silence lengthened, then, casually, she said, "Well, Earl Dumarest, it seems you are to be my guest."

There was a magic about her, an atmosphere of mystery and enchantment born in whispered tales heard when a boy in which creatures of grace would come to end all hardship and restore the comforts of forgotten eons. Promises and hopes now stirred to life by the strangeness of the city, the cerulean figure he followed along a path winding between scented bushes.

"My lady?"

Halting, she turned and looked down at him from where she stood high on the sloping path. Soft shadows deepened the blue of her lips and hair, turned the tint of her skin into misty smoke.

Dumarest said, "Where are you taking me?"

"To my house—where else?"

"And?"

"And then, Earl, you will entertain me."

A word which held several connotations but he said nothing as, turning, she continued to climb. A journey which carried them high, the path running between clumps of trees and flowering shrubs, vague figures half seen in the shadows. Figures which vanished when he tried to distinguish them, blending with the deepening gloom as darkness came to grip the painted sky.

The house was like the woman.

There was blue in it and silver and arches which spanned chambers and made opposing colonnades of smoothed and polished stone. There were tables which bore enigmas; vases of disquieting proportions, bowls of odd configurations, blocks of crystal in which elusive creatures were held in a deceptive immobility. The floor held elaborate patterns in geometrical mosaics. Lights shimmered from hidden sources and shadows moved in unrelated ways.

Dumarest paused as they crossed a room, halting before a bench littered with various tools. A mass of clay-like material rested beside a potter's wheel.

"Your hobby, my lady?"

"My name is Ursula, Earl. You will please me by using it. A guest should not be formal." The tips of her fingers rested on the wheel. "Yes, a hobby. One which bored me."

And so had been left to gather dust. But there was no dust and even the clay-like material looked as if ready for immediate use. Dumarest touched it, kneaded it, smoothed it again before following his hostess. How many other hobbies had she tried and abandoned and yet were kept in a condition of immediate readiness?

And where were the servants?

There had to be servants in a house like this. The windows were wide, winds blew and dust was inevitable. Dirt would gather and would be removed. Yet he had seen no sign of neglect and, aside from the half-glimpsed figures in the bushes outside, no sign of those who could be retainers.

"You swim, Earl?"

"Yes."

"And dance?" She smiled as he shook his head. "Fight then? You can fight?"

"Is that the duty of a guest?"

"A guest has no duty on this world, Earl. Only an obligation to entertain. Once I had a musician who played to me and once there was a woman who talked for hours of the men she had known. Both were boring. I need to hear things which are novel. But I am remiss! First you must be shown your room and, naturally, you would like to bathe."

The room was too large, too cold in its furnishings of blue and silver, the ceiling high and flecked with small but elaborate designs. The bathroom, in contrast, was warm and cozy with glinting mirrors and a deep, sunken tub which quickly filled with steaming water when he operated the taps.

Stripped, he soaked and thought of the house and his strange hostess.

An enigma, the house apparently had no servants and the woman apparently had no man. Neither made sense. She would have both even if only as a matter of comfort and yet seemed to prefer to live alone. Why pay so high for his presence? Why so desperate a need to be entertained?

Hot air blasted him dry and, dressed, Dumarest returned to the room with the wide, double bed. It was soft, the covers of fine weave, the sheets and pillows tinted the familiar blue. To either side of the bed, panels had been set into the walls, glowing at a touch, the light brightening and dying to the wave of a hand. A blue light. A blue-tinted woman. Blue sheets.

Why blue?

Dumarest turned to the window. It was a narrow arch, high, the panes small and set in thick bars which barely allowed the passage of his head and shoulders. Below he saw a sheer wall crusted with a vine thick with fretted leaves. To either side the wall was set with tinted bricks closely mortared. Above, the night had come into its own.

As yet it was not wholly dark but still it was dark enough for stars to have appeared and to be reflected in the waters of the lake below. Stars which burned like distant furnaces, hot, close, brighter than they would have been if this world had been Earth.

"Earl?" He heard the slight movement of the door, the rustle of garments as she crossed the room toward him on silent feet. Earl?"

He said, "I was thinking."

"Of the woman? Of Sardia del Naeem? You see, I know her name."

"No, not the woman."

"Of what then?" Impatience sharpened her tone. "Of the city? Of what is expected of you? Must I tell you again you have nothing to fear?"

"Nothing to fear but fear itself," he murmured. "Yet fear itself can kill."

"Earl?"

"A fragment of poetry I heard once," he explained. "I forget the rest. It was chanted by a wandering entertainer. He had a drum and with him was a boy who played a flute."

And there had been a fire with a dancing flame which had painted the scene with a ruby light. The smell of sweat had hung in the air together with that of dust and leather, oil and the warm, natural stink of animals and their ordure. A moment spent on a distant world and remembered for the scrap of poetry and the food which had warmed his belly. How long ago now?

He felt the touch of her fingers on his arm. "Hasel Ingram," she said. "He is usually credited with the poem though there is reason to believe it stems from a much older source. If you are interested I could quote you the accepted text."

"No, thank you." The past was dead and it was best to let it lie. "Is poetry another hobby of yours?"

"No." Her fingers closed on his arm. "Talk to me, Earl. We have time before dinner. Entertain me."

"Dinner?"

"Of course. On Ath we are not savages. Later we shall dine and I shall display you and there will be others you know. The woman, the captain, his navigator perhaps." Her shoulders lifted in the gloom. "Or perhaps not. We have seen too much of him and he can tell nothing that is new."

"And Tuvey?"

Again the shrug. "The captain is special. Now, Earl, why did you come to Ath?"

"I was looking for something," he said flatly. "A world with a similar name. One called Earth."

"Earth?" He saw the frown and tensed himself for the expected reply, the usual disappointment but, incredibly, this time it didn't come. "Earth," she said again. "How odd that you should know it. How so very odd."

He felt the tension of his stomach, the sudden hope which blazed through him to dampen his palms with sweat. With an effort he controlled his voice.

"You know it?"

"Earth?" In the shadows, the gloom of the night, her teeth shone with a pale luminescence between her parted lips. "Perhaps."

"Do you?"

She smiled at his insistence then looked thoughtful.

"Earth," she mused. "Its astronomical sign is that of a cross set within a circle. It is the third planet of its sun. The length of its equator is 24,901.55 miles. The equatorial diameter is 7,926.41 miles. The atmosphere is composed of several gases, the principal ones being nitrogen, oxygen and argon in amounts of about 78, 21 and 1 percent by volume." She blinked. "That is enough. Figures bore me. But yes, Earl, I know of Earth."

The room held the scent of oil and spirit, of paint and pigment, of bases and primers, of wooden stretchers and new canvas. A chamber which held all the evidence of long hours spent in painstaking creation. An artist who betrayed those even longer hours spent in the contemplation of despair.

"It's hard," said Cornelius. "So very hard. You get an idea, a concept, and you work on it until, within your mind, it is there in its final accomplishment. A work complete in every detail. Then comes the need to communicate and so the necessity of taking that image from the mind and setting it down on canvas. Of holding it with oils and colors. Of giving life to dead, unfeeling matter."

"I know," said Sardia. "I know."

"Do you?" His glance from the eyes deep-set beneath heavy brows was that of a mistrustful animal. His need for reassurance was the hunger of a child. "So few can really understand. They think that creation is simply a matter of application—as if constructing a work of art were a ditch which could be dug at any spare moment. They can't understand the importance of mood. The need for concentration."

The seeking and the soul-tearing exercise of what to put in and what to leave out. How well she understood. No dance could be given a personal interpretation without confronting the same devils which tormented every creative artist. The compromise. The limitations of the medium involved. The hopes and aspirations and, always, the sickening knowledge of failure.

Chathelgan had known it and had died by his own hand because of it. The ballet he had composed was acclaimed on a score of worlds but only he had known how far it had fallen short of its original conception. Far enough at least for him to have made an end. And Elmire who had gone insane when confronted with the limitations of the human frame when attempting a new interpretation of that most difficult of pieces, Myada's *Rhapsody of Dariroth*. She had seen him just before they had taken him away and even now shuddered when she remembered the ghastly emptiness of his eyes.

"I know," she said again. "I know."

"Yes," said Cornelius quietly. "I think that you do. Only an artist can appreciate the difficulties of another. To realize that to give birth to a child is no easier than to produce a new work. As a woman you should know that."

"No," she said. "I can only guess. I have never borne a child."

"But the principle is valid—all creation is an act of birth." His hand gestured at the walls of the studio in which they stood. "As this room is, in a sense, a womb. A concept Captain Tuvey found difficult to grasp when I spoke to him about it. But I forgive him. At least he introduced us."

And now she was his guest.

He found the thought strangely pleasing as he watched her study his work. The stack of canvases leaning against one wall seemed to attract her though many were unfinished and some little more than exploratory sketches. She lifted the one of the suspended man, still waiting for those few, final touches, her eyes traveling from the painting to his face then back to the canvas.

He said casually, "You like it?"

"It's superb!"

"But unfinished."

"You're joking, surely. This is magnificent!"

He smiled at the praise, childishly pleased to have won her approbation, entranced by the novelty of having knowledgeable criticism. Twice now she had mentioned business but each time he had dismissed the subject, altering the trend the conversation was taking. Later would be time enough for such matters; now he was eager to enjoy himself, to revel in her praise. It was odd how he had needed it, how little he had felt the necessity, now he sank into it as if it were a warm bath and he cold and tired and stiff from exertion.

"It isn't finished," he insisted. "The face requires a few touches. When I know what they are I shall apply them. Until then—" He broke off with a smile.

The smile made him appear younger than he was and at the same time frighteningly vulnerable. And yet he could be no younger than herself as the heavy lines running from nose to mouth testified. As the crinkles at the corners of the eyes. As the thinning hair and the slight sag of flesh beneath the chin. No child, this, no young and eager boy, but not old either. Just a man growing old and, perhaps, looking older than his years.

A thing she had seen before; often physical strength was the price which had to be paid for the flame of artistic genius, yet the face held a certain resolve. A determination to pursue the demon which plagued him; the creative madness which cursed all true artists. A thing they carried as a burden and a dread, hating it, fearing it, owned by it and totally possessed by it.

As Dumarest was possessed by his determination to find Earth.

Was there a difference? The pursuit of any objective was, in essence, the same. To attempt to convert a mental speculation into a tangible form in which it could be communicated to others and to chase the figments of a legend so as to gain proof that the legend was true—were they not the same? But while one could be seen and evaluated in terms of the objective attempted and success achieved, the other, until resolved, must always portray doubt. Yet a quest was a search and both men sought, in their own way, to find the same thing. The truth. The crystallizing of an inner turmoil. The creation of something neither could wholly understand.

A personal challenge, perhaps. An idea taken and set so that others could see. A painting finished—a world found.

She remembered Amil and what he had told her before he died.

"A man must try. Always he must try. If he does not he is nothing but a stone."

And, if in trying, he found only death?

"Sardia?"

Cornelius was staring at her and it was no time to be lost in introspection. She forced herself to smile as she crossed the floor and stared at what rested on the easel. A handful of flowers their stems spiked with thorns. Blooms which radiated an aura so that, suddenly, she could smell their scent as she had smelled the scent of bright blossoms when she had been a child and had yet to learn that no beauty is unaccompanied by pain.

"Sardia!" Cornelius's hand was on her shoulder, his face anxious as he looked into her own. "Sardia, what is it?"

"Nothing." She blinked her eyes free of tears. "Nothing at all."

She had found the source of a fortune—why should she cry?

Chapter Seven

Dinner was at midnight when the sun had long since died and the sky was ebon velvet dusted with gems. Stars which glittered with cold disinterest, curtains and sheets of luminescence occluded by the blotches of dust clouds, a haze which stretched like a coiled rope low on the horizon. A sky too bright to be that of Earth and one distorted by the electronic stresses found within the Rift.

Not Earth but a world holding the knowledge of where it could be found. A woman who must surely know the secret.

Dumarest looked at her as they stood on a balcony prior to joining the assembly. Tall, lithe, her body displaying her innate femininity, touches of reflected light turning her eyes into stars. Below them the city rested like a scatter of jewels cupped in a protective palm. Dull gleams ringed the lake and others shone from houses shielded by shrubbery, masked by trees. The air held the rich, warm scent of natural perfume.

A paradise and Dumarest said so. Ursula shrugged.

"You are easily impressed, Earl."

"I've learned to evaluate what I see," he corrected. "This could match the pleasure gardens on a score of worlds and has something even the Tyrant of Meld couldn't achieve with a fortune spent over a dozen years. His landscape lacks what you have here, a softness, a snugness—it isn't easy to put into words."

"A work of art," she said. "Can any two artists produce exactitude? Always there must be the minor difference of personal temperament. The subtle distinction which spells the difference between competence and genius."

"So the city was made," he said. "Built as a whole?"

"No. It grew and then was planned. There was much alteration and true harmony was not achieved until the Ohrm were removed. As for the rest, well, perhaps it holds a certain charm."

Her tone held condescension, her attitude was one of boredom, things which Dumarest recognized and he was quick to change the subject. Only a little could be learned at a time and to press too hard would risk losing all. The woman knew of Earth. She had knowledge he must obtain. The trick was to make her want to give it to him.

Now he leaned forward, hands resting on the parapet of the balcony, head tilted a little as he looked at the sky.

"Odd how the stars look in the Rift. I'd guessed they would be less plentiful and there could have been the glow of opposed energies. Have you ever seen them? Certain areas seem to trap and enhance natural radiation and, if there should be a fluorescent dust in the vicinity a spectacle can be obtained which holds true majesty. There is one close to Zekiah and another, better, which can be seen from Schwitz. You should make the effort to visit it."

"No." Her voice held impatience. "We do not travel from Ath."

"Never?"

"No."

A thing which she had hinted at before when, eager for entertainment, she had pressed him for details of the worlds he had seen, the adventures he had known. Stories for children, tales to pass the time. Always he was conscious of the similarity—a city built as to a whim, stories garnered from passing strangers, hobbies tried and discarded, projects started and abandoned. And no sight of any servants as if the things which were done were best done in secret loneliness.

And yet she was not a child but a woman vibrant with a woman's need. A thing he sensed as she moved closer to him, to rest her hand on his own, to tighten her fingers and dig tiny crescents with the blue-stained nails.

"Earl, on these worlds you have known, have you met many women?"

"A few."

"And have they loved you?" She smiled as he made no answer. "You are discreet but the answer is plain. Tell me, were any of them like me?"

"No." He turned to face her, his hand falling from beneath her own. "You are unique."

As every woman was unique, every person ever born, for no two could be exactly alike and every individual was a thing alone. A fact disguised as flattery by the tone of his voice, the direction of his eyes. And, even when a boy, Dumarest had known that to lie was stupid when the truth would serve better.

"Unique, Earl? You mean that?"

"As far as I can tell, Ursula, you are the most unusual woman I have ever met." And then, for fear she might mistake his words for irony, he added, "And one of the most beautiful. On any of a dozen worlds you would be a queen. On any of a hundred you would be known and loved and hated in equal measure."

"By other women?"

"Of course." He lifted the hand which had rested on his own and touched it to his lips. The fingers were cool, scented, smooth to his caress. "And, perhaps, by some men."

Her laughter was rich, throaty, the peal of bells. A

breaking of the momentary tension as she sought refuge in an appreciation of the incongruous.

"Earl! You are priceless!"

"Not quite, Ursula. It was fifteen thousand you paid?"

"Put into the common fund to be shared." The gesture she made diminished the sum. "A device invented by Garnar to add spice to certain moments. He is dead now but his work lingers on."

And would continue to do so as long as it provided entertainment. Dumarest said casually, "What are the Ohrm?"

"What!"

"You mentioned them." He gestured at the city. "When you spoke of achieving true harmony."

"The Ohrm," she said. "They are the ones who—the people who serve."

"A different race?"

"No. They are human. I—" She threw back her head, eyes misted. "The name is derived from Francis Ohrm who was elected spokesman for the passengers who traveled to Ath in the *Choudhury*. We are the Choud. The Ohrm are those who work and serve so that we can direct and control."

Servants or slaves?

"They serve," said Ursula. "They have always served. They tend the soil and grow the crops and do all things needing to be done under the direction of the Choud."

"For how long?"

"For always. No. Since the *Choudhury* landed on Ath. There was dissension and Francis Ohrm became more than just a spokesman. Punished, he died but his name lived on. Those who followed him became the Ohrm. They serve the Choud."

"Who do not travel?"

"No." Ursula blinked. "At least not to other worlds." Then, as a chime rose to hang quivering in the air,

"There is the dinner gong. It's time we joined the others."

They stood in a small cluster in a room graced with pendants of ice-like crystal all touched with an azure haze from lights shielded from direct view. A cold room with a floor of tessellated slabs all blue and silver. High arched windows framed the night, scalloped rims forming a surround for the stars. Natural pictures which would change as the hours passed to become flushed with the roseate light of dawn, the yellow blaze of day.

"Earl!" Sardia was among the assembly and came forward to greet him. "Earl, this is Cornelius. The artist we came to meet. Cornelius, this is Earl Dumarest. A friend."

If he noticed the slight hesitation he gave no sign but smiled and extended his hand and touched that which Dumarest had lifted. An old gesture and one common on worlds which had known strife; the empty palms visible proof of the lack of weapons. But when could Ath have known war?

"Earl. Sardia has told me about you. I hope that we, too, can be friends. Captain, I must thank you for my guest."

Tuvey had come to join them, his shoulder bare of his pet.

"Borol doesn't like too much company," he explained. "And festivities unsettle him."

"And that thing unsettles me." The woman Dumarest had seen before was at the captain's side and, while still revealing accumulated years, she no longer resembled a crone. Instead, metallic gints shone from lips and eyelids and darkness had hollowed her cheeks. Beneath her cunningly draped gown flesh swelled in enticing formations. "I'm willing to buy the man but not the beast. One day, perhaps, he'll agree to be bought for keeps."

"Maybe." Tuvey screwed up his eyes. "Who can tell, Etallia? If the price is right, who can tell?"

"Money!" The woman snorted her contempt. "That's all you think about. What is money against happiness? Stay with me and I'll give you more than you could hope to earn in the remainder of your life."

"And give me also what it could buy?" The captain smiled like a wrinkled gnome. "That, too, my sweet?"

"Greed! You lack blood, Lon Tuvey. In your veins is only money!"

"She's right," said Sardia as the couple moved away. "And the bastard isn't only greedy but cunning with it. I had a chance to speak with him about return passage. It's there if we can pay for it, Earl, but that's all. When I asked for the coordinates of Ath he laughed."

"Then ask your friend."

"Cornelius? He's an artist not a navigator."

"Someone must know." Dumarest stared at the woman, at her eyes. "There's something you've discovered. What is it?"

"I've found out how that cunning bastard tricked us, Earl. The passage and introduction, remember? Not one without the other. The long journey. The lack of coordinates. And Cornelius tells me that the *Sivas* is about the only ship that calls here. There's another, the *Mbotia*, but that hasn't called for months now. So it seems we travel with Tuvey or we don't travel at all." Her laugh was brittle. "He has us both ways. We get the paintings and pay through the nose to get them out. Then we pay again to return to Ath for more."

"No." Why hadn't she seen the flaw in her argument? Then he remembered. "I see—Cornelius refuses to travel. We can't take him with us."

"No, Earl, we can't."

"But why not? Damn it, all he has to do is to get on the ship."

"He won't." She shook her head at his expression. "Don't ask me why. An artist is a delicate creature and, like a flower, needs a certain combination of associations in order to produce his best. Maybe he feels safe here. Maybe it's something else. But I'm trying to change his mind, Earl. I'm trying."

And might succeed, given time; using her charm, her femininity, spinning a web with the lure of her body as women had done since the beginning of time. The old, age-old magic which so rarely failed. The love which, once instilled, made a man helpless to refuse.

Perhaps, as yet, she hadn't thought of that, but it would come if Cornelius continued to be stubborn. No one who had not learned how to apply the charm of her sex could have risen so high and she had been at the top of her profession. And no one who lacked determination could have gained such fame. That same determination had brought her to Ath and it would not be denied. She would win the artist; one way or another she would win, and if she did, would he mind?

Dumarest looked at her, sensing her nearness, her warmth, remembering the times of close proximity on Juba and in the ship. The times of passion. The words which had been spoken. The promises she had made.

And yet did anything ever last forever? And how could he blame her when he was doing the same?

"Earl?" She frowned, conscious that something had come between them, a chill not born of the cold decor of the room, the blue and silver so symbolic of ice and snow. "Is something wrong?"

"No. I was thinking of how to handle Tuvey." Of the need for passage and the greater need to learn more from Ursula as to the whereabouts of Earth. But he didn't mention that. Instead, he said, "Don't worry about it now. Just concentrate on Cornelius. Will he cooperate?"

"He'll let me handle his work, Earl. I'm certain as to that. As for the rest—" She shrugged. "Well, I've met stubborn men before. But we're up against time. If we

INCIDENT ON ATH

aren't ready when Tuvey decides to leave then we'll be stuck until he returns. Months at least."

Time in which enemies could smell out his trail. Time for the Cyclan to set a trap from which, this time, it would be impossible to escape.

Dinner was served in an adjacent room, one lit with diffused lighting, shadows thick against the carved panels of the ceiling, bright glows of warm color cast in patches over the central area. The table formed the three sides of an open square with the guests all sitting to face the space so formed. In it, a swirling mass of tinged mist, writhed a cloud of scented vapor which adopted new and peculiar shapes without end. A kaleidoscope of form and color, enticing, hypnotic.

"Debayo constructed it," said Ursula. "Before he grew interested in contacting the dead. Now he does little but squat before Hury waiting for revelations. Do you believe the dead can walk and talk as they did when alive, Earl?"

"On some worlds, perhaps."

"Do you know of one?" She shrugged, not waiting for him to answer. "The thing is ridiculous. Once dead, life is ended. All that can possibly remain is the residue of the electrical energy of the brain. A fragment of decaying energy spreading like the ripples on a pool into which a stone has been thrown."

"And yet, Ursula, if that energy could be isolated, trapped and amplified, what then?" A man sitting farther down the table twisted so as to face her. "Debayo has cause for his belief but I am certain he is trying the wrong approach. The method of using paraphysical energy was denounced in . . . in. . . ." His eyes went blank. "In the fifty-eighth year after First Landing when Wendis Cormagh demonstrated by impeccable logic that it is impossible to utilize a form of energy we can neither sense nor devise instruments to measure. To us, that energy, even if it exists, must be and forever remain nonexistent. His analogy was that of a blind man searching a darkened room for a black animal which was not present." He blinked.

"Karg's Ultimate, Corbey." A man called from where he sat at another leg of the table. "Sometimes known as the ultimate in absurdity and old before Wendis was born."

"But if Debayo should succeed?" Corbey paused and looked at the assembled guests. "Remember, contacting the dead would be only the beginning. Once that secret is learned then the dead will no longer be divorced from us. They will, in a sense, continue to exist. And that which does not die is immortal. That is what Debayo is after. Not words spoken to ghosts but the secret which will banish death forever."

An ambitious project but one in which Dumarest had no immediate interest. As talk flowed around and across the central mass of swirling vapor he leaned back and looked around. The guests were more soberly dressed now but still bizarre to one who had known the strict formality of High Families and ruling courts. No two gowns were alike and even the men wore clothing strictly to their personal taste. Blouses in a variety of colors, slashed, puffed, bound, ornamented, graced with fine tassles, decorated with intricate piping. Hair was streaked and blotched in rainbow hues, faces painted, eyes tinted, enlarged, enhanced with shaven brows and applied cosmetics. Among them he looked a drab fowl among peacocks. Even Sardia in her best gown of shimmering silk touched with ruffs of contrasting brilliance looked dull.

She looked at him and smiled then turned as a servant poured wine into her glass.

They had made an appearance for the first time and Dumarest watched them with interest. Small, delicately made, dressed in somber blue the color of lead, they drifted like wraiths, emotionless, soundless, unobtrusive.

INCIDENT ON ATH

Girls, he decided, or young boys, it was impossible to tell which. But they were nothing like the woman he had seen in the shadows on the path. Nor did they resemble the shapes he had seen lurking in the greenery. A different breed? The result of genetic selection which aimed at smallness and lack of sexual characteristics? A deliberate policy which ensured a supply of tamed and timid servitors?

One touched his arm as he moved and he felt thinness and fragile bone and saw wide, empty eyes which glanced at him once then lowered as if confused. A girl, he was sure. It had to be a girl, the contact had been female and the structure of the facial bone, the manner of walking due to a widening of the pelvis—it had to be a girl.

Or something which had been surgically achieved and which now had no sexual definition at all in the accepted sense.

Would they have done that?

He glanced at Ursula, leaning back in her chair, breasts prominent, mouth open to reveal the flash of teeth as she smiled. A lovely woman—but never had beauty been a guarantee of gentle behavior. Cornelius? No, he was too much an artist to subject flesh to such distortion, and yet cities had been burned in the name of art and men and babies set to die screaming for a musical accompaniment. How to tell? How ever to be sure?

"Your wine, Earl." Ursula was looking at him. "Is it to your taste?"

He hadn't touched it and she had noticed. A breach of etiquette in any such gathering. Now, lifting the goblet, he tasted sweetness and a cloying something which stung his tongue with acrid prickles. It vanished when he ate a cake containing tart fruits and a savory paste.

Meats followed, a variety of vegetables, compotes of fruit and nuts, wafers of spiced bread, cakes containing savory delights, sweets which stung and pastes which tantalized.

Then, the tables cleared of dishes, came the entertainment.

It was new to Dumarest's experience.

No performers made their entry and no musicians provided accompaniment. Instead, a man rose from where he sat, stepped into the writhing mist and began to sing in a cracked voice. Another followed him and jumped and twisted in a series of involved acrobatics, hands and feet vanishing into the mist which now had lowered to spread like an insubstantial carpet over the floor. A woman shrilled like a captive bird, another played an instrument like a guitar and harp combined.

Two men played at war.

Sardia laughed as they faced each other with blades carefully blunted. Knives which would have required an effort to cut butter and lacked the edge even to sever string. Mock blades used for practice, clashing as they met, ringing, cutting through the air as the men crouched and emulated fighters.

No, not emulated. Dumarest stared at them, his eyes narrowed, watching, evaluating. The feet moved as they should, the hands were correctly poised, the movements were those lauded by the classical school which was not necessarily the best. That title was reserved for the teaching which a man followed and won by following. But for the dilettantes the men provided a spectacle which they could appreciate.

Only Sardia mocked.

"Look at them, Earl! Ten to one you could take them both with only one arm. Twenty, you would gut the pair within five minutes!"

She had indulged herself with wine and was, while not drunk, not so sober as she thought. Her voice rose again over the clash of steel.

"They want entertainment, Earl! Give it to them!

INCIDENT ON ATH   101

Give them real blood and real pain! Give them something to think about!"

"Sardia!"

"Shut up!" She threw off Cornelius's hand. "Don't try to stop my talking. I've had enough of that. Talk is for fools. Words to entertain the passengers you've bought and carried home like toys. Well, I'm not a toy. And I don't entertain for nothing. You want real entertainment? Ask Earl to give it to you. That man can fight. He can fight as well as I can dance."

"Dance?" Ursula reared up in her chair. "You claim to be able to dance?"

"I make no claims." Sardia shook her head, suddenly aware of what she had done. "And I mean no offense. It was just that I was—"

"Bored?" Ursula's smile was devoid of humor. "You, bored? My dear, you don't know the meaning of the word. But you mentioned dancing."

"She's drunk too much," said Cornelius. "You have potent wine, Ursula. And the children were over-generous."

Children? Dumarest looked for the servants but they had gone. Had they been children? It was possible as most things were. Or was that just a euphemism?

"They do as they are ordered," said Elittia from where she sat at the captain's side. "But I am intrigued. A dancer, you say?"

"No. Not now. The wine—"

"Oiled your tongue. I understand. But once, surely, you could claim to know a little of the art."

Tuvey said, "Leave it, woman."

"Orders, Captain?"

"Sense. Drink some wine and sing us a song or something. Don't throw oil on a flame."

Advice she didn't follow and Dumarest sensed why. Jealousy showed in her painted face, in the glitter of her eyes, a flame which leaped and died but which he noticed before the bland mask was again in position.

"A dancer," she mused. "And, why not, a challenge? Now for the prize. This, perhaps?" Color glowed as she produced something from beneath her robe. "How about this?"

"My cube!" Sardia rose to her feet. "My music cube."

Bought be Tuvey from Ahdram as a gift to his hostess or as an item of trade. Used now by its present owner as bait.

"Your cube? Not yet, my dear, but if you can dance better than Ursula it is yours. You agree?" Then, as Sardia hesitated, her voice grew harsh. "You had enough to say before and were eager enough to boast of the prowess of your friend. Are we to assume that it was only the wine at work? If so, an apology—"

"No!" The old woman had been clever with a cunning learned from her paramour or one he had learned from her. Sardia fell into the trap. "I've nothing to apologize for. If it will entertain the company I will dance. And if the cube is a prize I will try to win it."

But not too hard, thought Dumarest. Remember you are a guest. Don't try too hard.

Advice she didn't hear and, if she did, would have ignored.

Chapter Eight

The cube itself provided the music, a susurrating rhythm which held the sensuous beat of drums and the thin, frenzied wail of pipes. A tempo gauged to the beating of a heart so that, as it accelerated, so did the organ with the consequent release of adrenaline, the heightening of emotional fervor until pleasantry verged into hysteria.

Exciting music in a theater where space separated the audience from the stage and those perfoming. Insane to use a tavern where the dancer could be touched and men carried weapons and had the will to use them. Unwise even in this house before such people when it was played in the spirit of challenge.

Ursula said, "Will you dance first, Sardia, or shall I?"

"As you wish."

"Music repeated could be boring to those having to listen and if we dance one after the other the second will have the benefit of learning the other's interpretation. You have no objection to our both performing at the same time?"

"None."

"It won't detract from your concentration?"

Sardia almost laughed her contempt. How little this decorated and decadent fool really knew. She remembered the old days when she'd waited for hours dressed in her leotards, moving simply to retain warmth and muscular suppleness, running onto the stage to join a dozen others all eager to catch the producer's eye. A system which encouraged each to give of his best regardless of what another might be doing. To concentrate, to think of nothing, to feel nothing, to be nothing but a creature wedded to music. To become nothing but a priestess of the dance.

"No," she said. "It won't detract from my performance."

"Then let us begin."

A touch and the music died, another and it recommenced as the women took up their positions. Dumarest watched as around him rose a tide of murmered comment. Ursula was the younger and therefore should be more supple. Yet the other, older, could have gained the greater experience. Yet few offered to bet and those seeking wagers all wanted to back his hostess.

A matter of diplomacy?

Dumarest doubted it, the expressions in their eyes were enough to eliminate that consideration. Some of them, like Elittia, wanted Ursula to lose yet seemed to have no doubt of her ability to win. Others, interested more in the excitement of the dance rather than the challenge, settled down to drink and watch and drink again as they yielded themselves to the pulse of the music.

Listening to it, Dumarest studied the dancers.

Ursula was splendidly lithe, her gown a cerulean shimmer, darker hues accentuating the swell of breasts and the curve of hips, feet naked in thin sandals, the nails darkly painted. Her hair was a cloud touched with silver, her arms supple vines with extensions; fingers which flexed as did her thighs, her calves, the arches of her feet. A symphony in blue.

Sardia wore white and flame, the rich darkness of her skin a glowing contrast, her hair oiled jet which caught and held the light and transmuted it into ripples of flame. A goddess from the olden times when men had ventured into woods to worship trees and perform sacrifices to ancient deities.

A woman now reflecting her pride in the turn of her shoulder and the sweep of her hair. Hair which fell in a cascade as she freed it from its restraints. Cloth which ripped beneath her nails as she tore vents in the skirt to display the long, lovely curve of her thighs.

And yet, still, she did not dance.

The music was still relatively quiet, a thin wailing as of pipes beneath shadowed trees, the sonorous throb of drums in answer, the melodies building, blending, forming mental images of empty spaces and secret groves, of fires left abandoned to flare in guttering winds. Of the sound of distant seas and the relentless beat of natural forces.

Ursula moved to the rhythm as if it were a wind which gripped her and dictated the shift of her feet, the play of her arms, the sway of hips and shoulders, the jerk and thrust of breasts and buttocks. Sardia moved like a reed at the edge of a pond rippled by a gentle breeze, her eyes half closed, hands hanging lax, only the shimmer of light on her hair revealing the small movements of her body. A woman almost lost in a dream. A dancer, remembering.

An auditorium filled with waiting men and women, the air tense with expectation, the orchestra settled, the stage dressed, everything ready to go. And she, the prima ballerina, about to dance the difficult role of Hilda in Obert's *Sacrifice to a Queen*.

The part of a harlot who seduced men with the motions of her body as she danced in a tavern.

One who had to dance, finally, for life itself.

Again she remembered Obert's instructions.

"No techniques, no tricks, no pretty spinning on the points. Ballet training teaches you how to dance—now dance. With your body, with your mind, with your emotions—dance!"

Then she had won a standing ovation, awards, fame. Now she could only win a cube.

The music caught her as she accepted it, yielding to it, letting her body become an extension of the beat, the rhythm. The ripple of muscle, the turn, the gesture, the sway of the hips all minor at first, all gentle, all helping to build the atmosphere and yet all hypnotic in their fascination.

Watching her Dumarest narrowed his eyes. Her face was different from that of Ursula and he glanced from one to the other, comparing, noting. The eyes half closed, the same but one held dreaming intent while the other had a detached glaze. And, too, Ursula's movements held a trace of deliberation as if she were listening to an instructor. A slight hesitation totally absent from Sardia's undulating grace.

Both interpretations of the music were basically the same—the rhythm left little choice. The beat was primeval and the dance was the same. Crudely done it would have been nothing more than a stylized depiction of sexual invitation; done as it was being done now it held connotations and subtleties which added layers of extra dimension to the elemental theme.

And Sardia was going to win.

There could be no doubt of it. Dumarest could see it, feel it, hear it as others shouted their approbation. It rose above the music now strident, dominating, driving the dancers as if it were whips. Thongs which lashed and sent yielding flesh into gliding postures, femininity exposed, displayed, flashes of curved limbs, hips which held the attention, gyrating, demanding, heating in wanton promise.

Ursula was accomplished but Sardia was transformed. A woman who had become a flame, dominating, destroying. One suddenly hurtful and cruel.

She had won, the yells had told her that, but still she continued to dance and each step, each movement, diminished Ursula's pretentions to ability. And still she continued, demeaning the other, belittling her, making her, by contrast, seem clumsy and totally inadequate.

"Enough!" Dumarest rose to his feet. "Captain, kill that music!"

The cube fell silent beneath Tuvey's hand as Dumarest strode through the wreathing vapor. Ursula ran past him, her face like ice, hard, cold, ugly, the tears in her eyes like glimmering pearls. Sardia turned toward him as he gripped her arm.

"Earl!"

"You bitch!"

"Why? because I did my best?"

"Because you didn't do enough." He stared at her, meeting her eyes, seeing in them a familiar expression. One mirrored on her face and which he had seen often when, after reaching the climax of love, she had relaxed in his arms. "With your training you were certain to win—you knew that. So why the hell didn't you use a little charity?"

"Charity?" She almost spat the word. "That is for monks and fools! I can't afford to be charitable. Can you?"

"I try."

"You try?" Her laughter was shrill. "Were you trying when you cut Yhma's throat? Was that your charity? No, Earl, when I fight I fight like you. I fight to win."

And, winning, looked lovelier than ever before. He felt her attraction, his response to the sensual warmth of her flesh, the invitation of her body. She was his if he wanted her, he knew that. His for now and forever.

But Ursula knew of Earth.

She had run like a hurt and wounded animal and as such would have sought darkness and a place in which to hide. Dumarest passed through the door she had taken, saw a wide passage pierced with windows, a door which opened on darkness. It led to a small garden now brilliant with starlight, leaves catching the light from the windows which added a ghostly luminescence to the pale silver from the sky. Dropping to a knee he studied the grass and saw faint traces crossing the sward to where a clump of bushes cast a deeper gloom. Thin branches pressed against him and his nostrils were filled with the sickly odor of nocturnal blooms as he stepped into the clump. Three steps and he turned; dressed as she had been, Ursula would not have taken the path he was following. Back on the sward he dropped again, frowning at the traces he now spotted.

The marks of footsteps but more than one. Some light and another much heavier. A trampled place and then a wider swath leading toward the edge of the terrace. He moved forward, fingers questing, searching for torn grass and ripped loam but finding only smoothness. No struggle, then, just a meeting and a departure. Rising he saw a scrap of something hanging from a twig.

It was fabric, fine, blue, a part of the gown Ursula had worn and probably torn free when she thrust her way past the bush. Dumarest followed and found himself on a narrow, winding path. Pale, silver starlight made an elaborate chiaroscuro as if filtered through leaved branches. Something moved in the shadows and his hand dipped to rise loaded with the weight of his knife.

"Ursula?"

Nothing and Dumarest moved silently to one side. If an enemy were lurking in the darkness he had given him advantage enough. Now he edged forward, sliding from patch to patch of shadow, left hand extended, the knife in his right poised to strike.

Something moved before him, a blur which became solid as he lunged forward, a shape which held substance and which struggled against the grip of his left hand. It took form as he dragged it into the starlight, silver gleams reflecting from the edged and pointed steel he aimed at the face.

"No! Please, no!"

A woman and one he had seen before. In the starlight he examined the square-cut face.

"Your name?" The knife moved closer as she made no answer.

"Pellia," she said quickly. "Please! The knife!"

Dumarest lowered it from where it had rested against her cheek, a spot of blood mute testimony to the sharpness of the point. A wound which would heal without trace but the threat of marring her beauty had been enough.

"I've seen you before. When the ship landed you were watching from beneath some trees. During the time of bidding. Why? What did you hope to see?"

"The bidding!" Her tone held contempt. "Why must you indulge their whims?"

"The Choud?" Dumarest eased his grip on the cropped hair. It was silken beneath his fingers, as soft as her voice, as the body he had touched beneath the blouse. A woman's softness overlaying firm muscle and well-constructed bone. As a child this one had never starved. "Why do you serve them? You do serve them, don't you?"

"I am one of the Ohrm, yes."

"And you serve?"

This time she made no answer but he needed no words. A servant, one who had learned to move quietly in the shadows and to watch and listen and learn—how little those who ruled realized how much they betrayed. And yet between her and those others he had seen in the house lay the difference between a pygmy and a giant. Were there others of as great a difference elsewhere?

She remained silent when he asked then shuddered as he lifted the knife.

"You would cut me? A woman!"

"I want answers. I'm looking for the mistress of the house. Ursula. Have you seen her?"

"No."

"People gathered on the lawn—yours?"

"A few. They come to watch but they did no harm. That I swear."

The truth or partly so, certainly they had done no harm to the sward and, had Ursula been attacked, she would have screamed or left traces he would have found. As it was he had only the fragment of cloth. Had she turned and gone the other way?

"Why are you watching?"

Again the silence, maintained even when he rested the knife against her cheek. For a long moment she stood rigid as the steel touched her flesh then, as it lowered, she released her breath in a gusting sigh.

"You didn't cut me."

"No, why should I?" Dumarest slid the blade back into his boot. "I'm just a vistor here and what lies between you and the Choud is your business. But take some advice, girl. When someone who threatens you asks a question give him an answer. It needn't be a true one as long as it satisfies." Then, without change of tone, he added, "Just why were you standing on the path?"

"Belain told me to. He—" She broke off, one hand lifting to her mouth. "You tricked me!"

"Yes. Is Belain your leader?" Her eyes gave him the answer. "Never mind. He set you to watch and to give a signal if anyone should follow, right?" Again he watched the flicker of starlight reflected from her eyes. As a conspirator she lacked practice. "What is going on?"

"You said you weren't interested."

"I'm not, just curious. Maybe I could help?" He waited then said, "Just as you wish. Are you sure you didn't see Ursula?"

"No, but I heard something before you came. Someone running up the path."

"A woman?"

"It sounded like a woman, yes."

Ursula, seeking heights and brightness and not depths and darkness, in that he had been wrong. Or she could have some private place in which she could sit alone to nurse her injured pride. To think and, perhaps, to plan her revenge. Sardia had been a fool and to delay longer would be to accentuate her folly with his own.

He said, "Pellia, tell me, has your mistress a favorite spot on an upper level? Ursula is your mistress?"

"No."

An assumption he had made without foundation—why should she belong to the household simply because he had discovered her close? And yet no establishment in a place like this was isolated; servants would talk, gossip would flow and the habits of one would be the knowledge for all.

"But you would know if she had such a place," he said gently. "Somewhere she would choose to be if hurt or upset in any way. I need your help. It is important that I find her and soon."

"Then ask another of the Choud."

"How would they know?" His hand fell to her shoulder, rose, a finger softly touching the spot of blood which marred her cheek. "For this I apologize. If you know where Ursula is to be found tell me and I will forget I've seen you here tonight. A bargain?"

"She is fond of heights," said the woman and her voice held bitterness. "It pleases her to look down on others. It pleases all the Choud. But if she has been thwarted you will find her on the upper terrace. There is a turret of stone surmounted by a crouching beast. In it she plots her revenge."

It rose like a ghostly castle in the starlight, a miniature palace set with fretted stone, dark with sprawling lichen, the beast above it a snarling, fanged shape radiating fury. Inside it was thick with shadows but the air held the taint of a familiar perfume and a section seemed lighter than the rest. A patch which moved and a face which caught the starlight and reflected it in the colorless semblance of a corpse.

"Ursula?" Dumarest stepped through the opening. "Are you here, my lady?"

"Why have you followed me?"

"I was concerned." The air held more than the odor of the perfume she wore, there was an acridity which spoke of insects and cobwebs and things which hid during the light of day. Imagination, probably, if she used this place then servants would have kept it clean. Or did she have a perverse attraction for mold and decay? "I came to escort you back to the house."

"So your harlot can gloat?"

"So she can apologize."

"Why?"

"She is a trained dancer, a prima ballerina. Almost her entire life has been spent in learning how to manipulate her body. The challenge was a farce from the beginning and one she should never have taken advantage of. It was the wine—she rarely drinks. And, too, I think she was more than a little jealous."

"Of me?"

"Can you doubt it?" Dumarest found a bench and sat down beside the woman. "Must I illustrate the obvious? You are younger than Sardia and she resented it. Your beauty also. Always until recently she has been the center of attraction and, in you, she saw mirrored what had been and would be no longer. Youth, charm, the ideal of men. Can you blame her for taking the only advantage she had?"

"The dance," said Ursula. "The dance."

"All she can do and even so her art is failing." It was no time to hesitate at a lie. "I watched you both. She bested you and you are woman enough to admit it, but in a year or two?" Dumarest shook his head. "A tree grows old and gains beauty with age. A woman gains maturity and can add to her attraction by the depths of her mind. But a woman who had nothing to commend her but muscular obedience—Ursula, she should be pitied, not blamed."

She said quietly, "I had planned to kill her."

And would have done and still could unless he could make amends. Sardia had been cosseted too long and had been forgotten if she had ever learned how vicious those born to wealth and power could be. The assassin, the subtle drug, the nerve-twisting poison, the killing bacteria—all were weapons easily at hand.

And who would mourn or revenge a lone traveler dying on a remote world?

"A guest," said Dumarest. "You would kill a guest?"

"Cornelius's, not mine."

"But still a guest of the Choud," he reminded. "At times, Ursula, we need to remember who and what we are. You are among those who rule on this world while Sardia is only a woman who acted unwisely while under the influence of wine. Already she regrets what she has done and wishes she could make amends."

"Such as an apology?"

An act she would detest but would do if he had to force her to her knees. Too much was at stake for him to pander to her pride.

"Yes," said Dumarest. "Even that."

"Even that?" Ursula lifted her eyebrows. "She means something to you?"

"We traveled together."

"And?" Her eyes watched his face; orbs filled with reflected starlight, pale ovals which glinted and looked as blind as glass. "Are you lovers?" She sighed at his nod. "So Tuvey mentioned to Ellitia. And yet you berated her for being less than kind. And you left her at the moment of her triumph when she needed you most. Your woman, Earl."

Dumarest said, "Not my woman, Ursula. Sardia isn't property. She isn't a slave."

"All women are slaves of their passion," she snapped. "As all men are victims of their ambition. It drives them like a goad and it can destroy them as love can destroy a woman. What is your ambition?"

"To travel."

"Why?"

"To search. To find."

"What? Happiness?" The turn of her head signaled her irritation. "What is happiness? Is it the contentment of a well-fed beast? Is it the lack of pain? Of hunger? Of doubt? Can you buy it? Make it? Find it in some forgotten place. Tell me, Earl, where can I find this precious thing?"

"In your heart, perhaps, Ursula. I know of nowhere else."

"Then why do you search?"

"For knowledge." He stretched and shifted so that his hand rested on his knee close to the hilt of the knife in his boot. A habit born of time spent in shadowed darkness with things which threatened from the gloom. "It pleases me to discover odd facts associated with various legends. The mythical planets, for example. You must have heard of them?"

"No."

"Worlds that are supposed to exist and yet which no one seems able to find." His tone was casual. "Worlds such as Earth."

"Earth is no myth."

"So I am convinced and I came to Ath in search of it as I told you earlier. And you reaffirm my belief. The details you gave were fantastic. Such precision. You could even know the spatial coordinates. If so then it would be possible to locate the planet." He paused, waiting, but she made no response. "Do you know the coordinates?"

She said, "Earl, let us not concern ourselves with that now. Tell me, and be honest, do you find me more attractive than Sardia?"

"Yes."

"Are you positive?"

"Yes." She was talking about physical beauty and he was thinking of far more than that, but even so she held an attraction which set her high as the dancer though in a different style. Hers was the loveliness of carved perfection while Sardia held the warmth of all humanity, the fire and the passion of seeding and harvest. "Yes, Ursula. Yes!"

She came to him like a scented cloud, her arms lifting to fold around his neck, her body shifting so as to press against his own, the twin mounds of her breasts flattening beneath the pressure. And she was fire beneath the ice, long muscles rippling, hips moving as her lips sought his own, teeth and tongue adding their own urgency to the message she was sending, the need she made no attempt to hide.

It was natural to respond. To return the pressure of flesh against flesh, to lift his arms and to send his hand caressing her hair, the fingers gliding through the silken strands to follow the curve of the skull, to feel the odd roundness set firm beneath the scalp.

"Earl!" Her lips left his to rise over his cheek in search of his ear. To bite as she voiced her desire. "Earl, I need you! I need you!"

As he needed her, not for the brief satisfaction of relieved physical tension but for the knowledge he sensed she possessed. A need greater than any she could ever have known or dreamed could exist.

"My darling! Earl, my love!"

There was blood on her mouth, dark in the starlight, and warm wetness on his face where more had run from his bitten flesh. A harlot's trick once played on him in a tavern and rewarded then in a manner which had left its mark. Now he could not afford to be other than gentle. Other than kind.

"Ursula!"

"You love me, Earl? You love me?"

He had traveled incredible distances, fought, killed, suffered hardship and almost died in his search for

Earth. A few pleasing words were nothing. Dalliance in this stone construction was nothing. Lies, promises, he would use them all to gain what he needed to know.

And then, abruptly, she stiffened.

"Ursula? What—"

"Be silent!" Her head tilted as if she listened to distant sounds. "Something is wrong."

She rose, suddenly cold, stepping to one of the slits which pierced the stone. Beyond rested the city, the lake, the field beyond. As Dumarest joined her, lights blazed from the houses and he could see running men head from the city, more on their way to the field. From behind the fence came little flickers of winking, ruby light.

They vanished in a gush of yellow flame.

A flame which limned the *Sivas* in harsh detail.

From somewhere below came Sardia's voice, high, shrill with shocked disbelief.

"The ship! My God, they've blown up the ship!"

Chapter Nine

The handler was dead, lying like a discarded doll on the ground, the ripped and charred clothing covering pulped bone and flesh. The steward had a broken arm and a cheek blackened by the blast. It had been coated with a soothing transparent film and he nursed the arm as he watched men busy in the light of dawn.

"I don't know," he said. "I was sleeping when I heard something. I moved toward the cargo hold and then it happened. A flash, a noise, and all the rest was confusion. I guess I was knocked out."

He had been found in an upper compartment and the negligence which left the door ajar had saved his life. The rest of the crew were unharmed; like the captain they had been guests.

"There was noise," said Dumarest. "Some firing from lasers. Did you see anything?"

"No. If there was noise I guess that was what woke me. But I didn't see anything. Just the flash as I told you."

Dumarest nodded. "Take care of that arm." He stepped toward the vessel as the engineer appeared at the head of the loading ramp. Like the hull in that section it was buckled but could be straightened with relatively little effort. The internal damage was more serious.

"The generator's damaged." Sharten wiped his hands

on the sides of his pants; like his face, his uniform, they were grimed with grease and soot. "The blast originated in the hold and blew the caskets to flinders. Well, we can manage without them, but the rest is another matter. The doors yielded and debris was blasted into the engine room. Some of it hit the generator."

"Can you repair it?"

"Sure, given time." Sharten eased his back. "It means stripping and checking the alignment and maybe a replacement. But it can be done."

"How long?"

"As long as it takes." The engineer scowled. "I'd like to get my hands on the bastards who did this. Eian was a good friend of mine."

"You think it was sabotage?"

"Cargo doesn't blow on its own."

"Cargo?" Dumarest frowned. "Were we carrying explosives?" He saw the shift of the man's eyes and turned to meet Tuvey's glare. "Well, Captain, were we?"

"That's my business." The man was blunt. "You've had the passage you paid for and now have no interest in the *Sivas*. Why are you standing there, Sharten? Get on with what needs to be done."

"Alone?"

"I'll see what help I can get. Renzi can give a hand."

Renzi was the navigator. Dumarest said quickly, "I'll find him for you, Captain. And you're wrong about my having no interest in the ship. I need passage away from here, remember?" He added, "And maybe I could help if you need it later."

"You worked on engines?" Tuvey grunted as Dumarest nodded. "Good. I'll bear it in mind. Now go and find that lazy bastard and tell him to get here fast."

The man was sitting in a quiet alcove in a house set close to the lake listening to a delicate melody and beating time with his hand. His hostess, a woman of ripe maturity, sat beside him and glared at Dumarest as he joined them.

The navigator said, "Tuvey sent you. He wants me to join him. Correct?"

"Yes."

"And you are wondering why I am not already at the ship. You see, Earl, how well I know your mind. How clear everything is. Lathrynne, my darling, be kind and pass me that little box."

"No, Renzi, you have had enough."

He smiled at the refusal and sat, listening, still beating time with his hand. A tall, thin, cadaverous man with a pronounced bulging of the eyes and hair he had trained to hang in a point over his forehead. One who had kept himself secluded during the voyage. One who now seemed vague and oddly unconcerned at the damage to the *Sivas*.

Dumarest said abruptly, "Did you know what was going to happen?"

"No. I have clear vision but not clairvoyance. Lathrynne?"

"No." She looked at Dumarest. "The alarm was given too late. Strangers were spotted close to the vessel and the guards were sent in with lasers. They must have startled the robbers or a shot went wild." She shrugged. "A thing to be regretted but accidents happen."

"How many dead were found?"

"Dead?"

"The handler was killed," explained Dumarest patiently. "There must have been others involved. The laser fire may have been poor but the blast must have caught some of those involved. How many?"

She frowned and threw back her head then said, "Three bodies were found. They are in the cold-store at the edge of the field." She blinked, life returning to her eyes. "Is Renzi really needed at the ship?"

"Ask him."

"No," said the navigator. "My task commences when

a course is to be plotted from world to world. If the ship is inoperable then I have nothing to do and so can take my ease. So, my sweet, if you will be so kind as to pass me that small box?"

She hesitated, looking uncertainly from one to the other.

Dumarest said, "Unless Renzi obeys his captain's orders there will be trouble. Tuvey is not a man to brook insubordination. The *Sivas* is crippled and needs to be repaired and it is the custom for all the crew to help at such a time." He added, speaking directly to the navigator, "Why argue about it? Cross the captain and he could abandon you."

"Abandon the navigator while in the Rift?" Renzi was amused. "You know better than that, Earl. And it would be no hardship to be stranded on Ath. All a man needs is an understanding friend and I have that, eh, Lathrynne?"

She said, "You'd better get to the ship, Renzi."

"You, too?"

"Just do as Tuvey orders. If you want to quarrel with him do it at the ship not here in my house." Her tone hardened. "I mean it. If you hope to be guested here again then do as I say."

Her hand fell on Dumarest's arm as the navigator, scowling, obeyed. After he had gone she stared at him, her eyes unabashed in their appraisal.

"So you're Ursula's guest. Does she please you?"

"She is an excellent hostess."

"And?" She smiled as he remained silent. "You don't have to tell me—she eats men alive. But in you, I think, she has found something novel. I've a mind to bid for you once she gets bored. A couple of days should do it. I'll throw in the navigator as a bonus."

Dumarest said dryly, "I'm sure he'd appreciate that."

"Oh, she wouldn't keep him, but there must be someone he could entertain." Her voice lowered a little, gained an added meaning, "And he was right about one thing. It would be no hardship for a man like you to be stranded on this world. I would support you for one."

Sardia called to him as Dumarest skirted the lake on his way back to the field. She came running to join him and fell into step at his side.

"How bad is the damage?"

"Bad. The engineer claims we need a replacement."

"Good." She smiled as he stared at her. "It gives us longer to do what we came for," she explained. "I'm going to meet Cornelius soon and I want him to finish some of the paintings he has. To me they are perfect as they are but you know artists, never satisfied."

"So I noticed."

"You're thinking of the dance?" She shook her head with brusque impatience. "Why bother about it? I won and that's all there is to it. Or do you think Ursula will want her revenge?"

"And if she does?"

"I can take care of myself."

"That makes two of you," said Dumarest. "Both superhuman. Renzi thinks he is indispensable and you think you're invulnerable. I'm hoping that neither of you learns how wrong you are."

"Renzi?"

"Is convinced the captain can't do without him. Tuvey may show him just how wrong he is. I'm hoping Ursula doesn't decide to teach you a similar lesson. It would help if you were to apologize. Tell her that you were drunk at the time."

"Me? Apologize to that spoiled bitch? Earl!"

"You want to make money, don't you?" He was harsh. "If you want that enough then you'll be willing to crawl if necessary. Ursula and Cornelius are close and she could have influence. She must certainly have friends. Think about it. Have you never seen how vicious a woman can be?"

Too often during the long climb up. Girls who had

been too brazen, too confident at the wrong time, too spiteful too soon. Little things had happened to them and some not so minor. An accident which had crushed a foot, another which had sent acid from a bursting container into a face and eyes, stomach convulsions at a critical time which had resulted in chances lost. And there had been fires, missed cues, broken promises.

There was no mercy in the jungle of the arts.

"I'm sorry, Earl. I just didn't think. Do you really want me to apologize?"

"Just be discreet. I've told her you weren't sober and more than a little jealous."

"You told her? When?" Her tone held anger. When you were making love to the bitch after you'd left me?"

"You think that?"

"Does it matter to you what I think?" She halted to drag at his arm, to turn him to face her. "Does it?"

"No," he said flatly. "Not when other things are more important."

"Like the feelings of that blue strumpet?" Rage accentuated her beauty with a simmering fire. "Well, to hell with you, you bastard!"

She ran from him down the path, past the misted fountains, the early swimmers who sported in the water. One, a lithe young girl, stared after her and laughed. Another, a man, shrugged and dived as if he had been born into the medium. Dumarest made no effort to follow. Given time she would get over her anger but it would take much longer for the trouble to vanish from the field. Unless the *Sivas* could be repaired he would be an easy target for those who would come in search.

He passed the vessel on his way across the field. The ramp was still down with men working on it under the navigator's direction, the sound of hammers loud on the air, fading as he reached the blank edifice of the coldstore. The sound died altogether as he passed inside.

The place was bleakly functional, a chilled enclosure in which perishables could be kept, a part of it now converted to a morgue. Dumarest walked toward it, little echoes murmuring from beneath his boots, a faint crunching of broken ice which ceased as he halted at a roped enclosure. Beyond the barrier rested three trestle tables loaded with covered bundles.

Stepping over the rope Dumarest went to the one on his left, jerked back the cover and looked down at a ruined face.

Once it had been young and sleekly handsome but now it was a torn and ravaged travesty of a human visage. One eye was gone, the cheekbone smashed, a mess of pulp where an ear should have been. Dried blood matted the hair and the mouth had been ripped by splintered teeth. The body, carrying fragments of burned and torn clothing, followed the same pattern. The hands had vanished, the forearms, the elbows converted into ugly stumps. The intestines hung like a tangle of soiled rope. Dumarest touched the head before turning to the next.

It was a young woman and a freak of the explosion had left her almost unmarked. Only an edging of blood at the lips, the scarlet suffusion of the eyes and the telltale signs in the ears told of the forces which had taken her life. Her hair was of a reddish gold sheen he had seen before.

As Dumarest went to touch it a voice said, "It's soft, isn't it? And she was beautiful, wasn't she? Too beautiful to be left alone?"

"Too beautiful to be dead." Dumarest gently ran his fingers over the hair and moved a tress from where it hung over the staring eyes. He tried to close them but rigor had set in. Replacing the cover he looked at the woman standing against the wall masked by the shadows. One he had seen before on a path dappled with starlight. It was obvious why she had been standing a lonely vigil. "Your sister?"

"Yes," Pellia stepped forward, small crunching sounds rising from beneath her sandals, ceasing as she halted at Dumarest's side. "I was watching in case—" Breaking off she said bleakly, "A beautiful girl. She was to have been married next month. To Heyne." Her hand made a gesture toward the remaining bundle. "At least they died together."

The boy, also, was relatively unmarked about the face but the lower portion of his body had been wrenched and broken by the impact of the blast and a scrap of metal had almost buried itself in the chest. Dumarest jerked it free, looked at it, threw it back as he drew the cover over the body.

"Why?"

"Why was I standing here? Alline is still beautiful even though dead and the Choud are bored. Some of them might want to—"

"Not that. Why did they do it?"

"Do what?" Pellia looked blank. "I don't understand what you mean."

"Don't give me that, girl! She was your sister and you had to be close. Why did she want to rob the ship?"

"She didn't."

"She was there with the others. Why?"

"An accident." Pellia looked from side to side, her eyes those of a trapped animal. "It must have been an accident. She and Heyne had gone out to look at the ship and became involved in what happened."

"And the other one?" Dumarest jeked his head at the first corpse he'd examined. "What about him? Did he accompany them? A spare lover, perhaps? Was your sister hard to satisfy?"

She said furiously, "You filth! Don't defame the dead!"

"Then don't take me for a fool. All three were close, the injuries prove that. Therefore they had to know each other and lovers aren't usually eager for company. The first man was holding whatever it was that exploded. Heyne was close to him and my guess is that your sister was standing behind him. His body protected her from obvious injury but her internal organs were ruined by the shock wave. Three of them, all close, all working in harmony. No accident, Pellia, and you know it." Then as she made no answer he added quietly, "How many were really killed? How many were hurt?"

"Why do you ask these things? You are not of the Choud."

"No."

"Then why be so concerned?"

"My concern is with the ship." Dumarest glanced past the woman to where the doors stood shrouded in gloom then, taking her arm, led her toward them. "But why are you so afraid? An accident, you said, and who can help an accident? It was natural for Alline and Heyne to have wanted to see the ship. Natural also for them to have helped unload if asked. Who could guess at what would happen? Then, after the explosion, those left unhurt ran and took their injured with them. Their other dead, too?"

"No, only those hurt."

"And needing attention. Are they getting it? Do you have drugs?"

She said bitterly, "All drugs are dispensed by the Choud."

"And you daren't go to them for fear of being arrested and interrogated." Dumarest nodded. "I understand. Do you trust me, Pellia?"

"I'm not sure. You kept your word the last time we met but this is different. Why should I trust you?"

"Because I'd like to make another bargain with you." They had reached the doors and Dumarest paused. "I'll get you some drugs and do what I can to help the injured and, in return, they can do something for me. They can give me a name. A single name."

He felt her sudden tension, the abrupt strain of aroused suspicion. "Which name? Whose?"

"The one who allowed them to unload the *Sivas*."

The ship looked much as he had left it but the ramp was straight now and the buckling of the hull smoothed. The workers had gone and the immediate area around the vessel was deserted. Dumarest paused at the foot of the ramp, looking back toward the cold-store. Pellia was nowhere to be seen but she would be watching him, hiding in the greenery or standing immobile against a mottled patch of stone with, perhaps, her head in shadow. Good places to hide if you knew anything about camouflage and Dumarest guessed she had long since learned that it was movement and not shape which attracted the eye.

Within the ship the air held a peculiar taint of char and burned gases, of seared insulation and the reek of dispersed chemicals. The hold was a mess, the floor littered with the fragments of the caskets used to carry men and animals, coolants evaporated and leaving blotched stains, the mechanism of the apparatus itself a jumbled ruin. Dumarest touched a bulkhead and looked at the grime on his finger. Chemical explosive would have left such a trace, one of tremendous power and, apparently, poor stability.

He moved and touched another portion of the inner hull this time at a place close to the port. Again he examined the grime and found it apparently identical with the other. Wiping away the dirt he crossed the hold and paused at the door beyond. It led into the engine room and he could hear a succession of small sounds; metallic scrapings, a rustle, a drone of muttered curses, a ringing. Glancing inside he saw the engineer where he crouched before the dismantled bulk of the generator. The man was alone.

Another door led to the passage communicating with the cabins and leading to the salon and then on up to the control room and the normally restricted portions of the vessel. Dumarest glanced into the cabins as he trod softly along the passage. In one of them the steward lay on a bunk, light glistening from the transparent film on his cheek, his arm held awkwardly away from his body. As Dumarest entered the compartment he opened his eyes.

"Earl! What are you doing here?"

"I came to see how you're getting on. How's the arm?"

"It hurts."

"How did they treat it? With Staders?"

"I think so." The fingers flexed as the steward moved; visible proof of the metal splints which had been riveted to the bone on either side of the break to hold it firm. "I was out when they treated me but I guess that's what they must have done. The wound is sore, though, and it aches like hell."

"Let me have a look." Dumarest pursed his lips as he examined the wound. It was a neat gash, the only evidence of the surgery which had opened the flesh to permit the splints to be fitted, now neatly held by sutures which would become absorbed into the body. Gently he touched it to either side, pressing, easing the pressure as the man sucked in his breath. "That hurt?"

"Like fire. You think it's infected?"

The flesh was bruised and would have been rendered tender by the force of impact and the later treatment, but Dumarest didn't mention that. The man had a low pain level and it was easy to enhance his fears.

"It could be. Let me check again." This time he pressed harder and caused the man to grunt. "That's bad. It shouldn't hurt as much as that. Just once more."

"God!" The steward was sweating. "What's going to happen, Earl? I could lose the arm, become a cripple. Regrowths cost money I haven't got."

"Take it easy, man. It isn't as bad as that. I can fix it." Dumarest held out his hand. "Just give me the keys to the medical cabinet and I'll get what's needed and do what's to be done. Or do you keep your drugs in here?"

A chance, on small ships stewards tended to maintain

their own medical supplies. The *Sivas* follower the custom.

"In that drawer. You'll find the key in the one below." The steward wiped his glistening forehead. "There isn't much."

An understatement. Dumarest looked at the neat rows of packages all bearing recent dates. He selected ampuls and loaded a hypogun.

"Give me the arm." He fired local anesthetics directly through the skin and fat into the area around the wound, the hiss of the driving air blast a sharp sibilance. "Better?"

"Yes." The steward flexed his fingers. "You think that'll do it?"

"For now. Is Renzi or the captain around?"

"Damned if I know. Renzi should be helping Sharten and I guess the Old Man's busy in the town." The steward winced as he moved. "Are you sure you gave me enough?"

"Give it time. What's the latest on the repairs?"

"Nothing. Sharten's still not sure if he can manage without a replacement. Check with him if you want to know more. Me, all I want is to get rid of this damned pain. You sure you've done enough?"

"This will take care of it." Dumarest fired the hypogun at the man's throat. "In three seconds you'll be asleep."

A sleep which he made sure would last by trebling the dose. Pocketing the hypogun Dumarest helped himself to various packages from the drawer, then, locking it, replaced the key where he had found it. Outside the cabin he closed the door then turned to face it as footsteps sounded from the higher reaches of the passage.

"Earl?" Renzi came toward him, his eyes vague. "A surprise to find you here, but life seems to be filled with many surprises of late. What can I do for you?"

"Nothing, I came to see how the steward is getting on." Dumarest rapped on the door. "This is his cabin?"

"It is." The navigator pushed open the panel. "And he appears to be asleep. It would not be kind to wake him, my friend. You were not, I trust, thinking of seeing the captain?"

"No."

"You are wise. He is not in the best of moods. His pet has had the bad grace to destroy itself though I must admit I am not displeased. Only the manner of its passing disturbs me." Renzi smiled and steadied himself with a hand pressed against the bulkhead. "Did I say disturb?"

"What happened?"

"Borol is dead. The spined, horrible thing is no longer with us, but in dying it left its mark. You see, Earl, for some unaccountable reason, the creature decided to chew and tear its way into the radio. Perhaps it needed to eat and if so was doing well until it formed a bridge between two sources of power. Now, cremated, it is no more." Renzi smiled again then added, "And neither is our means of communication. Earl, my friend, I would advise you to find an amiable host—we could all be a long time on Ath."

Chapter Ten

From where she sat on the dais Sardia said, "I'm getting stiff, Cornelius. May I move now?"

"Later." He was being unfair and knew it. Setting down his brush he said, "I'm sorry, of course you may move. I've been thoughtless but time has passed so quickly. Forgive me?"

"For what? Asking me to model for you? That is a compliment. I shall live forever immortalized by your genius."

"You exaggerate."

"No."

Deliberately she drew in her breath before rising to stand, to stretch with arms upraised, the light from the great window adding richer tints to the smoothness of her flesh. She was nude aside from a drape around her hips, the proud contours of her breasts now catching the glow from the painted, sunset sky, the brown of her skin accentuating the shimmer of diverse color. Beauty personified, he thought, watching her. The loveliest creature he had ever seen. Why was it so hard to capture her image in paint?

He looked at what he had so far accomplished and fought the inclination to tear the canvas from the easel and destroy the mockery it contained. Were these lines and daubs the best he could do? Did those scrawls and dabs depict the loveliness which now stood before him?

Was his talent so small that he was unable even to convey what was real to the world where he had thought himself a master?

"No," she said quickly as his hand lifted. "No!"

"It's useless!"

"It's a beginning." She moved with her dancer's grace to stand at his side, eyes narrowed as she studied what he had done. "A good beginning."

Nonsense and she knew it—who could tell what a good beginning was in the realm of art? A scrawl which would not dignify the literary status of an idiot could be nursed and nurtured to form an epic when handled by a master. A few lines, a scatter of notes, an insignificant chord and a symphony could be born. And even though the canvas held little of apparent worth the feeling was there, the striving, the reaching out and the aspiration.

As she was the inspiration.

"It doesn't do you justice," said Cornelius. "Nothing created by human hands could ever do that. You are sublime in what you are. The ultimate of perfection; flawless in every way."

"I am a woman, Cornelius."

"So?"

"No woman is without fault and never make the mistake of believing you have found one who is. May I dress now?"

A request he could not refuse and it had been polite of her to ask. A subtle way in which to let him know that he was the master as well as the host. A courtesy which he recognized and appreciated as he appreciated her willingness to pose for him. Had he asked or had she offered? He couldn't remember and the details didn't matter. It had happened. For the first time it had happened.

And, for the first time, he was in love.

Sardia could sense it as she dressed, recognizing the atmosphere, the slightest tension which ruled his every movement; the little gestures quickly controlled, the words which came a little too fast and were too plentiful; masks for their real meaning, the thoughts they covered. A familiar situation—always there had been those crowding her dressing room entranced with the glamor which accompanied her. Love born of illusion, those experiencing it confusing the performances for the reality. A madness which left most unharmed but which, badly handled, had caused pain and death to others.

Would he kill her if she should refuse him?

She said quietly, "Cornelius, don't misunderstand me, but I think it would be better if I were hosted by someone else. Ursula, perhaps."

"That bitch? No!"

"Would she have me if I asked?"

"Why should you do that?" He imagined he guessed the reason. "Is it because of Dumarest? Are you jealous of him?"

"No."

"No?" His eyes held her own. "I wish I could be sure of that. You traveled together and have been lovers. I—"

"Did he tell you that?"

"No." Me blinked at the interruption. "But it's true, isn't it?"

"Does it matter?" Her shrug gave the measure of the importance she attached to the subject. "I was thinking of your work, Cornelius. I feel I am a distraction. Don't misunderstand me, you are a genius, but with you art must always come first. This portrait, for example, you look at me too often and for too long."

"You are beautiful!"

"As is a flower, the sunset, the flight of a bird. Beauty is in the eye of the beholder. But your work holds more than beauty. There is an added dimension which must be maintained." The ingredient which set him above others and would make his work fetch fantastic prices. The thing he must not lose and she sensed that it had its roots in pain. She said, "Have you used live models before?"

"No."

"Because they create a conflict?" She knew the answer before he nodded. The fact at war with the impression, eye straining against brain, the observed data clashing with the subconcious awareness of what should be. "Cornelius, you are not alone. Many artists produce their best work in isolation. They store up impressions, ideas, methods of treatment and then, when finally ready, they close themselves in a world of their own and become lost in the creative process."

He said flatly, "Are you telling me that you don't want to see me again?"

"Of course not!"

"For the sake of my paintings? The markets you spoke of? The money you said I would make?" His voice grew bitter. "What is money to me? What can it buy that I don't already own? Happiness? Only you can give me that. Sardia, don't leave me, please!"

He was a small boy crying in the darkness. One begging for the comfort she was too much a woman to refuse. A step and she was close to him, her arm around his shoulders, her free hand running over his hair as, smiling, she looked into his eyes.

"I won't leave you, Cornelius."

"You promise? You'll stay here with me?"

"Until the ship leaves, yes."

"And then?"

"I'll return, of course, often. Or better still, you could come with me."

"No."

"Why not? What is to stop you? Oh, I know, the Choud do not travel." She masked the impatience the answer had given, one she faced again. "But all the Choud? Couldn't you, at least, be spared?"

"No. It isn't that. I—" He drew in his breath and

stepped away from her and said, looking at the window, "Why can't you stay here on Ath?"

"Business, Cornelius. I have to attend to the display of your work and achieve the recognition of your genius. I explained all that."

"Agents could handle it. You could send the paintings to friends who would do as you direct. Dumarest could take them. You trust him?"

"Yes."

"Where is he?"

"I don't know. I left him at the lake this morning. We had a quarrel."

"Dumarest." Cornelius threw back his head and his eyes veiled. "He is with the Ohrm." He blinked. "Why should he be there? Ursula has been looking for him and he has neglected the obligations of a guest. Sardia, I—"

"No." She sensed coming danger, a decision she would have to make. "We'll talk later. I've a slight headache and I'd like to rest for a while. The fact is I'm not used to posing and it was a greater strain than I imagined."

Her smile absolved him from blame. "Please, Cornelius, be a darling and understand."

"Later? You promise to talk later?"

"Of course." How often in the past had she handled just such an incident? But this was one suitor she dared not rebuff too harshly. "Later."

Alone, Cornelius looked at the easel and the work it supported. A waste; the marring of pristine canvas for no good purpose. The outline was wrong, the pose, the position of the head and arms. A woman seated at her ease and dreaming as she stared through a window. A lovely woman but there was more to beauty than the contours of the skin. And, sitting there, what did she see? What was she thinking?

And where was the suffering? The pain?

It guided his hand as he reached for the brushes. It

INCIDENT ON ATH 135

decided the pigments used, the direction and intensity of the strokes, the fury of his application. Outside the sky darkened as the night conquered day, shadows adding their mystery to the vista beyond the window. Lights glowed to banish the inner gloom and still he worked on, sweating, his face taut with strain. A man obsessed. One in torment as, again, he entered his own private hell.

The path was uneven and twice Dumarest stumbled before mounting the final slope to stand on the summit of the ridge and stare down into the bowl which held the city. Behind, hidden from view and unable to spoil the jewel-like perfection of the terraces, the homes of the Ohrm sprawled in an untidy growth which reached toward the plains and the mountains beyond. A collection of low-roofed dwellings, clean and functional, but set too close and lacking the individual charm of those owned by the Choud.

"It's beautiful," said Pellia at his side. "So beautiful."

"No."

"But, Earl, how can you say that?"

"It's pretty," he corrected. "But that's all. It has no life, no warmth. Listen." He held up a hand, starlight glinting on his fingers, his nails. "No laughter. No noise. No sounds of people at play. No quarreling, no shouting, no passion."

"And no pain." Her tone was bitter. "No burned flesh and dying men."

Too many men—those who had used the lasers hadn't all missed. Dumarest thought of those he had tended: men with charred holes penetrating vital organs; wounds which had been cauterized by the beams which had made them, each wound now a repository of pain. One had been burned across the eyes, another hit in the groin, a third lacked a lower jaw.

He had done what he could, injecting antibiotics, giving the balm of unconsciousness, easing pain and setting bones shattered by the blast. Rough surgery when skilled attention was needed but the best he could do.

And, in return, had learned almost nothing.

"I'm sorry, Earl." Pellia tore a leaf from a shrub and shredded it between her strong, white teeth. She had stayed at his side as he had worked and had grown close. "Was it important to you?"

"It doesn't matter."

"All they know is that the handler allowed them to unload the ship. Then the guards arrived and the shooting started. One of the boxes must have been hit."

Hit to explode and kill those holding it and the handler too. The blast had spread to fling debris against the generator. Facts Dumarest was aware of but other questions remained to be answered.

He said, "Those wounded trusted you more than they did me. They could have told you something in confidence. There was more than one box?"

"Yes, Earl."

"And most of them had been moved before the guards arrived?"

"So they say, but not all of them saw the inside of the ship. They collected the boxes from the ramp."

"And took them where?" He reached out and gripped her shoulders as she made no answer. "We made a bargain, Pellia. I was to tend the wounded in return—"

"For a name. Well, you have it. The handler was the one who gave them permission to unload."

"And who ordered them to go to the ship?"

"No one!"

"Are you telling me that a group of men just decided to meet at a certain time and go to the ship and unload it all without anyone having any idea as to what they were to remove or where to take it? Someone must have given the instructions, Pellia. Who?"

"You're cheating!" She strained against his grip. "That wasn't in the bargain! Let me go!"

"Was it Balain?" For a moment longer Dumarest held her then dropped his hands. "Balain," he said thoughtfully. "The one who set you to watch on the path. Is he your leader?"

"What is that to you? We made an agreement—your help for a name. Well, you have it. The handler ordered the unloading of the *Sivas*."

A dead end. He had bought a certain amount of cooperation but now his credit was exhausted. Turning, he moved down the path toward the city. It was narrow and twisted across the steep slope, a rarely used way and one mostly used by the Ohrm. Bushes flanked it and cast deep patches of darkness. From one of them, lying ahead, came a faint rustle.

Dumarest slowed, eyes searching the starlit area. The path wended, curved, passed below him at the foot of a steep incline dotted with shrubs and toothed with boulders. Ahead lay the bushes, three clumps merging to throw the path into darkness. From one of them came the rustle. A soft breeze could have caused it or the stirring of some nocturnal creature but there was no wind and the animal which had caused the sound had done so for no apparent reason.

Dumarest took two more steps, planting his boots firmly on the path, creating an impression of steady progress then, abruptly, turned and was racing down the slope. It was too steep to maintain balance and he doubled as he fell, turning himself into a ball as he rolled over the ground. A shrub lashed at him, a boulder scraped his shoulder, then he had reached the path, had risen and was running down it as from behind came the pound of feet.

Two men who ran silently after him and another who stayed high and sent the cry of a bird into the night.

A signal answered from lower down the slope.

Fools, had they remained silent he might have run into the trap; alerted, he was on his guard. Dumarest slowed, looked to one side and saw a clear expanse protected by a serrated wall. To jump over it would mean a long drop and the risk of a broken leg. To continue would be to run into the waiting men, to be caught between them and those closing the space at his rear. To remain still was to present a target and, already someone was shooting at him.

He heard the thrum of a released string and the spiteful hiss of an arrow. One which flashed through the air where he'd been standing to sink quivering into the ground. Short, thick, feathered with metallic glints; a bolt from a crossbow. A primitive weapon but as effective as a laser when used by skilled hands at close range. As effective but not as fast; such a weapon took time to reload.

Turning, Dumarest ran back up the path, weaving as he ran, body stooped low, his hand reaching for the knife in his boot. Three men, two close, one who could have a weapon and one more sophisticated than a crossbow. An unknown number now behind him but they would hesitate to move and be slow to fire for fear of hitting their companions. The ones now close would have to be the first targets. Hit them and the darkness would shield him as well as those lying in wait.

Dumarest dodged, sprang to one side, heard the hiss of the air as a club swung at his head then dived in, the blade extended in his hand, the point hitting, ripping, slicing across a muscular torso to open a long gash across the ribs. A thrust converted into a cut as his momentum carried him past the man, the knife dragging behind, turning, jerking forward, upward to hit the club-loaded arm, to cut across the inner flesh, to sever muscle and open the arteries and release a shower of blood.

"God! I'm cut! Wilkie!"

The second man who was too slow and died, eyes startled, throat opened so as to present a grinning mouth to the stars.

"Wilkie! Flavian!" The voice came from above,

changed as the speaker saw the two sprawled bodies, the figure of Dumarest running back up the path. "You, down there! Get him!"

He stepped into the open, one hand lifted, a ruby beam guiding the fury of the laser. Dirt smoked to one side and a bush flared into burning life as Dumarest threw himself to one side beneath the shelter of a boulder. He heard the pound of running feet and turned to see two men running from where they had lurked. One carried a crossbow.

"Hurry!"

The man with the laser was impatient and so was careless. He came to join the others, the weapon lifted in his hand, overconfident of the advantage it gave him and forgetting that a gun is only as good as the man using it. Crouched against the dirt, Dumarest heard the pound of the man's footsteps as they neared his hiding place. A stone rested beneath his free hand and he lifted it, threw it far to one side, slipping to the other side of the boulder as it landed. The men fired as he rose, standing awkwardly, aiming too high and trying to correct his aim. He was still trying as Dumarest, coming from behind him, drove naked steel into his spleen.

A blow which killed as quickly as a bullet in the brain. The man slumped, soundless, the laser falling from his hand to hit the boulder and go tumbling down the slope. Dumarest followed it, hearing the spiteful hiss of an arrow and feeling something hard slam hard against his thigh as, catching up the laser, he rolled and turned to fire.

"Masak?" A voice from higher up the slope. "Is that you, Masak?"

Another voice, higher, younger. "Masak is dead."

"Dead?"

"Knifed." A pause and then, "Let's get out of here! Move!"

An old trick to persuade an enemy to reveal himself and Dumarest waited, immobile where he sat, only his eyes shifting as they searched the silvered gloom. Finally he moved, diving into patches of darkness, moving as silently as starlight, as fast as dancing flame. Stealth and speed which carried him down the slope to where a house sat like a gem in a cup of tended greenery. To a woman who had waited too long.

She was like a tigress, a barely contained creature of seething emotion, pride and dignity alike affronted by his apparent indifference.

"You are my guest, Earl. As such you have certain obligations. If they do not please you then be honest enough to say so. An arrangement can be made."

She was cold and it was hard to think of her as the passionate woman he had held in the turret, yet beneath the icy chill he could sense the masked fires she fought to control. Fires of anger and revenge rather than those of desire and all the more dangerous than those of simple need.

"I beg your pardon, my lady, I was detained."

"Do you mock me?" She had been striding across the floor, moving with a lithe grace, turning to move again. Now she halted and stared her accusation. "I am not your lady. I am your hostess."

"And I was detained."

"Tending the Ohrm. Nursing men who deserve to be eliminated. What did you hope to gain, Earl? Another woman to fall into your arms? Another victory?"

"Information." He was curt. "Doing the job you should have done and should be doing. You, the Choud, your guards. Guards!" He made no effort to mask his contempt. "Where are they when needed?"

"When needed they are summoned."

"By whom? The Choud?" Dumarest looked down at his soiled clothing, the place on his thigh where the arrow had ripped the plastic from the protective mesh. "A pity none of you were around earlier this evening. They could have saved some lives."

INCIDENT ON ATH

"You were attacked?" Abruptly she was concerned. "When? Where?" She tilted back her head when he'd told her then blinked. "Guards have been alerted and will comb the area. It is monstrous that the Ohrm should have the temerity to venture so close to the city when they have no duties here. And to have attacked you—Earl, doesn't that show you what manner of creatures they are?"

"I know what they are," he said coldly. "Human beings."

"Animals."

"Servants through no fault of their own."

"Slaves who want to be free."

"What?" She stared at him then shook her head. "Earl, for a man who has traveled you are strangely innocent. Isn't it obvious to you that some people are more gifted than others? That some are meant to rule and others are destined to serve? It is the natural order of things and has been so on this world since the First Landing. The Choud make the decisions and the Ohrm obey. Anything else is unthinkable."

"To you, perhaps, but others may have more active imaginations." Dumarest looked at the laser he had found then handed it to the woman. "Do you recognize this?"

"A standard pattern," Ursula barely glanced at it. "The same as used by the guards." Then, as she recognized the implication, she added emphatically, "No, Earl, you were not attacked by the Choud."

"Then how explain the gun?"

"It was stolen or—" She broke off as her eyes misted. "No, that is not the explanation. No weapon has been stolen either from the individual or the armory." Blinking, she explained, "This is a small world and we have only one city. There is no need of a large stock of armaments and none are missing. Hury is certain of that."

He frowned, recognizing the word, the second time

he had heard it. When had been the first? At the dinner before the women had danced when someone had mentioned Debayo who sat before Hury.

Remembering, he said, "Ursula, when you mentioned Debayo, you said he sat before Hury. Where is it?"

"Don't worry about that now, darling." Her smile was warmly possessive. "We are to visit for dinner and you have yet to bathe."

A change of mood but warmth was better than hostility and far more welcome in someone from whom he needed to gain information. Soaking in steaming, scented water, Dumarest reviewed recently acquired items of knowledge. The Ohrm, Pellia, the men who had attacked him for reasons he could guess. He had asked too many questions or those of the wrong kind and they had taken him for a spy. A natural mistake but one which had almost cost him his life.

"Earl?" Ursula had come to join him and stood at the edge of the tub dressed in nothing but a thin robe of shimmering azure. It fell to reveal the unadorned lines of her body as she leaned toward him. "I've come to massage your back, do you mind?"

For an answer he extended his arms.

Chapter Eleven

The dinner was held at the house owned by Etallia and this time Renzi was invited. He sat with his hostess at a round table dressed in the center with a mound of succulent dainties served to add climax to the meal.

"Food!" Tuvey puffed out his cheeks as he selected a fruit with a striped rind. "That's the trouble with being guested on Ath. A dinner every night and food enough for an army. Better than the basic most of us grew up on, eh, Earl?"

"That's right, Captain."

"Food and more food." Renzi was becoming expansive though he had said little during the meal. "Things to eat and things to taste. Nice things which come in decorated boxes. Nice women who provide them. Gorgeous ladies like my Lathrynne." His hand fell from her shoulder to glide with slow deliberation over her breast. "To live on this world would be a pleasure. To die on it—"

"Would be a pain," snapped Lathrynne. "As you are getting to be." She pushed aside his crude embrace. "Is there nothing else, Etallia?"

"A novelty Lon bought me. Not the music cube—that has been handed to the victor of our recent little contest—but something as amusing. A globe of living motes which fight and die to breed again on the bodies of the fallen and so wage perpetual war. A gambling device, so I understand, no one can guess the ultimate end of any combat. Come and see it. And you, Rattalie? Cominaria? Wynne? And you, naturally, Ursula." Her smile held pure venom. "As a compensation. Perhaps you can win on something which requires no personal effort."

"The bitch!" Sardia dug her teeth into a crusted ball of inner sweetness. "Does she work at it or does it come to her naturally?"

"A game." Tuvey set aside his fruit. "I've watched it for years. Each time I visit Ath they are at daggers drawn. Not just those two but all the Choud. The product of boredom—if they had to sweat they would not hive time for minor feuds."

"Years, Captain?" Dumarest selected a pair of hard-shelled nuts and crushed them together in his palm. "You have been visiting here for so long?"

"Years." Tuvey fell silent and stared blankly at the center decoration. Then, "Years," he said again. "I make it a regular run. The guesting alone is worth it."

"The guesting and the rest." Renzi sank back into his chair. "Tell them of the rest, Captain. The true joy of Ath." His smile was that of a clown. "Tell them of the tekoa."

"Watch your tongue!"

"Why? What is the secret? His women will tell him if we do not. She will tell him and show him, too, if I read her correctly. And I know how to read a woman, Captain. I can read one as I can read a spectrum gauge or a digital output. Ursula is in love with our late passenger and a woman in love will give a man her world."

As she had promised when, locked in his arms, they had both surrendered to passion lapped by the steaming water of the bath. Scented vapors had accentuated their desire and the water, far from cooling, had added fuel to her ardor. But the world she had promised was not the world he sought and still she had not told him how to find Earth.

INCIDENT ON ATH 145

"Earl?" Sardia touched his hand. "Don't let him upset you."

She had misread his introspection and her eyes were anxious. They cleared as he smiled and shook his head.

"I was just thinking. What news as to the *Sivas*, Captain?"

"Little and all bad." Tuvey rose. "I should be there now, helping Shartan. We should both be there." He glanced at the navigator, who shrugged.

"The obligations of a guest, Captain. And what do a few hours matter?" He, too, rose. "Let us join the rest. Sardia?"

"Later."

"When your host arrives?" Renzi winked. "Or did you exhaust him this afternoon? Cornelius seems far from strong."

She said with cold ferocity, "Talk that way to me again and I'll rip out your eyes. I'm no cheap harlot to take the filth from your sick mind. Wash out your mouth, man, before someone fills it with broken teeth."

"You?" He backed as she rose and lifted one foot to send it against the hand he lifted, the fruit it contained. A kick which turned it into a messy pulp. "I'd forgotten, a dancer knows how to use her feet."

"Her nails, too—you wouldn't be the first I've taught to behave." She looked at Dumarest as the navigator left with the captain. "That should have been Ursula. I'd have ruined her pretty face."

"And paid for it."

"Perhaps. Cornelius—"

"Is weak and you know it."

She said patiently, "I wasn't going to say he would protect me. But we have been talking and he told me a lot about the Choud. They settled here from some other planet. Three ships forming a convoy which reached the Rift. One was destroyed when it ventured into an energy vortex. The *Choudhury* landed here on Ath. The other, the *Khawaja*, became separated and they lost contact."

"Three ships?"

"Two, Earl. One was lost in the vortex." She added, "He talked while he worked. I was posing for him."

"And?"

"We just talked, Earl, not that it's any of your damned business. You let me know exactly where I stand with you. It's Ursula first and all the time, isn't it? You're lovers, aren't you?"

Dumarest said, "What else did he tell you?"

"Cornelius? Not much. He said you were with the Ohrm today."

"How did he know? Did you tell him?"

"How could I?" She stared into his eyes. "I didn't know where the hell you'd gone after we'd parted. I— well, I had to bathe my eyes. Dust, I guess. Then I went to see Cornelius and he asked me to pose and so I did."

"Any visitors? No?" Dumarest frowned. "Then how did he know where I was? When he told you, how did he look?" He nodded as she answered. "A little vague as if he were listening to something. Have you noticed it before?"

"Not that I remember Why did you visit the Ohrm?"

"To learn what I could."

"About what?" Sardia caught at his arm. "We're partners, Earl, remember? Leaving everything else aside, we have an agreement of mutual help. Is there anything I should know?"

"He said bluntly, "The *Sivas* was sabotaged."

"The explosion? That was an accident."

"Maybe, but I wasn't talking about that. On the face of it Tuvey's pet chewed its way into the radio and destroyed both itself and the installation. Couple that with the damaged generator and we're in a bind."

"How?" She frowned at her own stupidity. "Of course! Unless the engineer can repair the engine we'll be stuck. Tuvey can't radio out now for another ship to bring him replacements. But why should anyone do a thing like that?"

"You tell me."

"Renzi? He likes it here but would he sabotage the ship to stay? Tuvey? He's the captain and can remain as long as he likes. The handler? No, he's dead. The steward? Doubtful, he hasn't the guts or the brains. The engineer? Why?" Shrugging, she ended, "Hell, it's anyone's guess. There's no one else."

"There's you."

"Me?" Her laughter was genuine. "Earl, have you gone out of your mind? The quicker I get those paintings back to real civilization the better. I've Cornelius eating out of my hand and every hour spent here now is an hour longer to wait for a fortune. But you?" Her eyes narrowed with speculation. "Maybe you don't want the ship to radio out. The woman? A need to hide? Afraid Tuvey might send a message to be relayed back to Juba that the man they were looking for is to be found here on Ath? Was that it, Earl? Did you wreck the radio?"

"No."

"You could have. There isn't much you couldn't manage once you put your mind to it." Her hand dropped to his own and she stared at him, abruptly serious. "Earl, I'm jealous and I'll admit it, but I'm not a young girl and I know that certain things happen." She remembered Cornelius and her own manipulations. "Sometimes they have to happen—all living is a matter of compromise. But if you're in trouble and I can help?"

"Thank you."

"I mean it, Earl. Just ask and it's yours. Anything. I owe you that."

He said firmly, "You owe me nothing. All debts have been paid."

"Some debts can never be paid." The fingers of the hand resting on his tightened with a warm intimacy which diminished the importance of mere physical association. Then, conscious of the stinging in her eyes, she said, "We're business partners and shouldn't be getting sentimental. There's no profit in sentiment. Earl, I need cheering up. Isn't there anything interesting you think I should know?"

"Only one thing," said Dumarest dryly. "We're sitting in the middle of a revolution."

"The Ohrm? Rebelling? Impossible!" Casavet threw back his head and laughed. He was a big man who had helped himself plentifully to wine and was a stanger to Dumarest. "My friend, you must surely be joking." He wiped his eyes with a scrap of lace-like fabric. "A revolution! Here on Ath!"

Tuvey said, "Are you sure, Earl? If you're not, it was a damned stupid thing to have said."

"I'm sure."

"How? You read it in the stars? Listened to a message carried on the wind? " The captain's scowl left no doubt as to his disbelief. "You've been on this world just over a single day and you think to know more than those who live here? Who rule!"

"There is an old saying," said Lathrynne quietly. "The husband is always the last to know. I don't take Earl for a fool and only a fool would have made such a statement unless he had grounds for believing it to be true." Her voice hardened a little. "You have data?"

"A ship damaged by explosives accidentally detonated. Why were they being carried and who ordered the unloading?"

"Captain?"

"Explosives are a normal cargo for any vessel operating as a trader and touching a variety of worlds. As for who ordered the unloading, I guess the handler did."

"The man who is dead and now cannot be questioned." Lathrynne glanced at Dumarest. Without discussion she seemed to have become the head of the impromptu interrogation. The child-like servants who had been discreetly present during the meal had vanished. "Well?"

"Some of the explosives were unloaded and taken to a predetermined point. And there was a laser which didn't belong to your normal armament."

"Which could have been left here by a previous visitor," pointed out a man.

"And given to the Ohrm? Exactly." Dumarest looked from one to the other. "I notice you avoid the subject of where the expolsives could have been taken."

"If any were taken." The man raised the objection. He was young with purple hair and neat in puce and emerald. "The first box to be unloaded could have been detonated."

"Doubtful but possible," admitted Dumarest. The young man seemed to have adopted the position of a devil's advocate and, like Lathrynne, had done so without discussion. "But some of the Ohrm were hurt in the blast and they refused to come to you for help. That in itself would be suspicious on the majority of worlds I have visited. When the people fear authority there is usually a good reason. As far as I can tell, you don't seem to be unduly harsh."

"We treat the Ohrm as if they were children," said a woman. "Children to be loved and protected."

"We are of the same roots," said another. "We landed on the same vessel—surely, you know a little of our history?"

"We ask only that they should obey," said a man. "And we ask that only because they lack the knowledge to govern themselves."

Ursula said blankly, "Why should they hate us? They should be happy."

"As you are?" Dumarest waited for an answer and when none came added, "I'm not defending the Ohrm. I don't give a damn for their condition or imagined grievances or supposed cause. But I am a guest and, as you've mentioned before—" He glanced at Ursula. "—A guest has certain obligations. In my experience it is to defend the people and the property of those who have given him hospitality. I have given you warning and that ends my obligation. If you refuse to heed it then that is your business. Now, with your permission, it is late and I am tired."

"Earl! Don't leave!" Ursula turned to the others. "At least let us probe the possibility. Lathrynne? Khurt?"

The young man nodded. "Of course."

"Yes," said Lathrynne. "Is there general agreement? Etallia? Casavet? Rattalie?" Nods answered as she called names. "So what do we have so far? Explosives which may have been taken from the *Sivas* and hidden. Men injured by a known event who refuse to ask for treatment. A gun which must have been smuggled or stolen by a servant some time in the past. An attack on a guest which he fortunately survived. And?"

"A feeling," said Dumarest. "A conviction."

"That a revolution is imminent? How imminent? Tomorrow? Next week? In a month? A year?"

"If I could tell you the exact time and the manner of the insurrection," said Dumarest dryly, "I wouldn't be a guest but a prophet."

"Or the leader of the insurrection itself." Lathrynne nodded. "A good poiont. It was unfair to try and pin you down. Is there anything else?"

"Names. Wilkie, Flavian, Masak. They were three of the men who attacked me."

"And who are now dead. A pity. Did they need to die?"

"They wanted to kill me." It was answer enough. Dumarest added, "But they would have had associates and they could be found."

"And persuaded to talk. Of course, but there is doubt as to their identity. Many of the scanners in the homes of the Ohrm are no longer operating or have become erratic."

Scanners? Dumarest had seen none or, if he had, had failed to recognize them for what they were. As easy mistake; such instruments could be small and masked in a variety of ways. But scanners presupposed a central operations room where data could be evaluated and correlated. Another item to add to the rest but as yet the knowledge was of little use.

He said, "Are any scanners installed in the homes of the Choud?"

"No." Lathrynne looked puzzled. "What would be the point?"

A question Tuvey answered. "None. Earl, you probe too deeply. It would be wise to remember that you are a guest on this world."

"As you are, Captain," reminded Dumarest. "But I present no danger to my hosts."

"Are you saying I do?" Tuvey stepped forward, fists clenched, face ugly. "You accuse me? Do that and I'll leave you here to rot."

"As you did Balain." Dumarest saw the captain frown, glanced at Renzi and saw his blank expression. "You know him?"

"No. Damn you, Earl, you—"

"I wasn't accusing you, just stating a fact. The *Sivas* is a prime factor in the revolution. It has been used to bring the insurgents arms and explosives. It could even have supplied their leader."

"Balain? No."

"How can you be certain, Captain? Men have been smuggled before."

"Not on my ship." Tuvey looked down at his hands, unclenched them, then halted the automatic movement of one toward his empty shoulder. He frowned, missing his pet, an irritation exploded into anger. "Damn you for a fool! Why can't you leave well enough alone? This is a nice, pleasant world and I want to keep it that way.

That's why I keep it secret and why I'm reluctant to carry passengers. Now you've spoiled it with your talk of revolution and arms and explosives. There was an accident, that's all, and—"

"Men tried to kill me."

"So you say. But what reason could they have had? A woman?" Tuvey glanced at Sardia then at Ursula. "Another woman? Didn't you have the sense to leave the Ohrm alone?"

"Did Balain?"

"To hell with Balain! He's just a name you picked up from somewhere. I've never seen him and wouldn't know him if I did. If he exists at all he's some crazy fool chasing dreams."

"No," said Dumarest. "He's not crazy and he's not chasing a dream. What he wants he can get. And what he wants is to end the rule of the Choud."

Casavet laughed. He laughed as he had at the first mention of the rebellion, jowls quivering, tears streaming from his eyes. A man convulsed with genuine amusement.

"Earl, my friend, you will kill me with your jokes. Balain destroy the Choud? One man?" He broke into fresh peals and ended gasping and dabbing at his eyes. "The thing is inconceivable. You don't know—how could you? You don't understand. If you did you would realize how incredible the concept is. One man, even the entire Ohrm, couldn't harm us. The Choud cannot be overthrown."

"You are wrong," said Dumarest. "And you are making the biggest mistake which could ever be made by a ruling class. You consider yourselves to be invulnerable and that your rule will last forever. If history has anything to teach us at all it is the fact that such conviction is the prelude to inevitable defeat."

"Nonsense!"

Dumarest shrugged. "It's your world."

"And a strong one."

"Strong?" Goblets stood on a nearby table; fine-stemmed containers of engraved crystal with fluted rims and delicate curves. Dumarest selected one and held it between his outstretched fingers. "Strong," he said. "I could stand on it and it would carry my weight if I chose how to position it. It's beautiful, too. As strong and as beautiful as your world." He opened his fingers and, as the goblet fell to shatter on the floor, added, "And as brittle."

Chapter Twelve

Tuvey was gruff. He said, "Here you are, my lady, safe to your door. No revolutionaries can get you now."

Sardia forced herself to smile at the weak joke. Cornelius, despite his promise, had failed to join her and the captain had escorted her home. Now he stood, a little awkward, arm lifted as his fingers searched for his missing pet. He noticed her eyes and lowered his hand.

"I miss him," he said simply. "Borol wasn't much to look at but he was company of a kind. The sort which doesn't make demands. You know?"

"Yes, Captain, I know."

"A man needs a companion in space. Something or someone who can be close. Some men travel together most of their lives but I've never met anyone with whom I could be that friendly. It makes a difference."

To a man and to a ship—the *Sivas* had been cold with a chill owing nothing to the lack of heat. Sardia said, "I mustn't detain you. Your hostess will be looking for me with daggers if she thinks I'm keeping you from her side."

"Etallia?" His shrug was eloquent. "We're used to each other and that's about all. She knows better than to be jealous."

"No woman knows that, Captain."

"And not all women can tolerate a man as ugly as I am." He was stating a fact, not fishing for a compliment. "I know it and she knows I know it. Knows, too, that I can't afford to be independent while on Ath. That's something Renzi has yet to learn. The stupid bastard!"

"His mouth?"

"His damned carelessness. Borol didn't like him—he used to tease the beast when I wasn't around. I would have kept him with me but Etallia wouldn't hear of it. So I left him in the control room. I guessed he liked to be put on guard and he was snug enough in his box but Renzi had to go after him. He must have tormented the poor creature and it tried to run." He added savagely, "He'll pay for a new radio and compensate me for the loss of my pet before I get rid of him. I swear to that!"

"The radio was Renzi's doing?"

"Yes. He confessed earlier this evening while we watched the gambling. The fool was high and thought it a joke. I'll give him a joke. If he ever lands on this world again it won't be on my ship." Tuvey swallowed and lifted his hand in a brisk salute; one learned half a galaxy away when young. "I've kept you standing out here long enough. Good night, madam."

"Good night, Captain."

Politeness which held a cold formality, the formality itself a sense of security. Rules by which people chose to live; a custom which could be appreciated and a discipline which provided support as well as barriers. Did the Choud have something similar? Were there areas of privacy into which none could intrude without condemnation?

Why had Cornelius broken his word?

The answer was in the studio and she paused at the door seeing the figure slumped in the chair before the easel and feeling a sharp anxiety before she noticed the rise and fall of his chest, heard the susurration of ragged breathing.

"Cornelius!" He was asleep, sunk in a numbing exhaustion, not even the slap of her palm against his cheek enough to arouse him. "Cornelius, wake up!" Again she slapped the flaccid cheek. "Wake up!"

"Who—" He stirred, one hand lifting, the fingers thickly smeared with paint. "What—"

"Wake up!" Spirit stood close at hand. She gushed it on a rag and held the rising vapors beneath his nostrils. "Cornelius! Please!"

He stirred again, the hand blindly groping, eyelids twitching. She thrust the rag beneath his nose, the sting of the spirit against delicate membranes an added stimulus, then, as he reared a little, kissed him full on the lips.

"Sardia!" He rose higher to sit upright, his arms closing around her. "Sardia, my darling!"

The kiss had been a wind kindling latent desire to a dancing flame. She felt it as she retreated, sensed her own response, and rose to step backward well away from his reach.

"You promised to join me. What happened?"

"I was working and must have lost track of time." He ran a hand through his hair. "God, I feel exhausted. The box. Pass me that box."

She handed it to him and watched as he opened it to reveal swollen yellow pods. He lifted one and slipped it into his mouth, biting, leaning back as he chewed. The transformation was amazing, within seconds the muscles of his face had firmed, the flaccidity born of fatigue washed away together with his fatigue.

"Tekoa," he said. "At times it helps. Helps you to relax, that is. Helps you to drift and think and plan and see everything in bright colors." Fatigue had given way to euphoria and he sensed it. With an effort he added, "I don't use it often."

"Would it matter if you did?"

"Perhaps not but—" He broke off, giggling, becoming abruptly sober again. "I'm sorry. It hits you like this sometimes. The contrast—don't worry about it. I'll get over it soon."

She said nothing, staring at the easel, the canvas it supported, the picture he had painted since she had seen him last.

Herself?

She stepped closer, looking at the figure, a female, seated on plain boards, one knee lifted, the face resting on the summit of the curve. A woman dressed in a soiled costume with tinsel wings drooping like the tattered vanes of a butterfly, the body-garment accentuating the tired drag of breasts and stomach. A dancer as she could tell from the shoes. And it was so real.

Leaning closer she could smell the greasepaint, the odor of dried sweat, the female exudations caught and held by the fabric of the costume. Feel, too, the rough boards beneath her buttocks, the aching fatigue, the depression. The performance was over, the audience gone, the lights dimmed and now she sat alone. A woman who had danced the part of an angel. One now fallen. One soiled and dirtied and conscious of her state.

Herself?

She had sat before the window, tall, gracious, the light warm on the smooth contours of her body. Her head had been high, the chin uplifted in proud grace, the lips carefully arranged in a smile—and Cornelius had been unable to freeze the picture with his genius. Instead, after she had gone, he had created his own interpretation. A dancer, soiled, degraded, disconsolate —was that how he saw her?

She looked even more carefully and more details sprang to life. The barely seen lines on the face which gave it an air of corruption. The eyes which told of cynicism. The lips which told of standards lost never to be regained. Even the curve of the fingers had been made to resemble claws avid in their greed. A woman who had sold herself for ambition. Who had accepted compromise and the use to which her body could be put. The face of a cheat, a liar, a thief, a whore.

Her face.

Sardia turned and ran from the studio, crying, feeling naked and ashamed.

The guard was young, confident of his ability and impatient to be getting on with the job. The leader of a score of others, all young men of the Choud taking their turn of duty and excited at the prospect of interesting action.

Dumarest said, "Be sure and check the walls, floors and roof. Don't forget the outside of the roof as well as the inner rafters. Check every item of furniture. If you find anyone who insists on staying in bed then move him and search the bedding. Even if they are sick move them just the same. You understand?"

"We know what to do."

"I hope so. Look into cupboards, cabinets, cradles. Check toys and boxes and privies. Don't forget the people; watch their eyes as you search. A glance could give you a lead."

Again the man said, "Leave it to us. We know what to do."

A confidence Dumarest didn't share. Though young and confident they would lack experience but he had done all he could. As they moved off into the darkness Ursula said, "If you're wrong, Earl, I'll be the laughing stock of Ath."

"And if I'm not?"

He saw the answer in her eyes, the sudden warmth which accompanied the touch of her hand. She would be grateful; no member of the Choud wanted to be host to a fool, and in her gratitude she would tell him what he needed to know.

"Earl, let's go inside. It's getting chill." She shivered beneath the cloak she had flung over her shoulders.

"Pre-dawn adentures are all right for men wearing heavy garments but I'm not fond of hardship. Let us go into the house and you can share my bath and we can talk of your past exploits."

"I'd rather be with the guards."

"I know. You men are like boys. You want action and incident and the fun of giving orders. And you want to be proved right, Earl. But there is nothing you can do more than what is being done. All exits from the area have been sealed, the region cut into sections and already the first divisions are being checked. If explosives are there the guards will find them."

Dumarset frowned, the decision to search had been recent, how had men been moved into position so quickly? He hadn't even heard them alerted.

Then, remembering the crossbow, he said, "I hope they aren't stupid enough to underestimate the Ohrm. They have weapons which can kill."

Weapons they were willing to use. Dumarest heard the scream as they moved across the lawn toward the house and felt Ursula stiffen at his side. It came again, a long, wailing shriek which ended in an ugly gurgle. The sound torn from a man with punctured lungs who had tried to run and had fallen to scream his pain before blood had filled his throat.

"They were waiting," he said. "And ready."

"For what?"

"The guards, the search, they expected it." He looked up toward the ridge, seeing moving points of light against the sky. "They could be coming down here to attack the city."

"No, those lights belong to the guards. They will protect us." She clung to his arm. "No, Earl! Stay here with me!"

"And listen as they die?" Another scream had seared the night. "Don't those fools know enough to stay under cover?"

She followed him as he ran up the winding path leading to the summit, falling back, joining him as he slowed and halted at the crest. Guards stood in line, armed, portable lights standing dark but ready and aimed toward the homes of the Ohrm lying sprawled below.

"Get those lights working," snapped Dumarest. "Keep them high in order to illuminate the roofs. Aim them lower and you'll make easy targets of your companions. What happened?"

A man glanced at Ursula who nodded.

"The search had started and seemed quiet enough, then some women started acting up. As we pressed into another section one of our men was hit."

"With what?"

"An arrow. He fell and we didn't know what had happened at first then another got it. You may have heard his scream."

"And?"

"Two more followed, one is dead and the other close to it. We got them out and scattered." He squinted as the portables flashed into life. "We were going to wait until dawn."

"That's what they wanted you to do." Dumarest looked at the vista revealed by the lights. Some of the roofs had crude parapets built of stone and bags of dirt. "Were any other weapons used aside from the crossbows?"

"No."

"Which doesn't mean they haven't got any. Right, have the men split into pairs and operate as teams. One to cover the other—you understand?"

"Yes, but wouldn't teams of three be more efficient? Two to cover and one to move?"

"And if one gets hit?" Dumarest didn't wait for an answer. "Use pairs. They can double up if necessary but each knows that he has to rely on the other and will be that much more attentive. Keep those lights on the roofs to dazzle snipers if they are present. Have men watch the strong points on the houses but don't fire unless they are occupied. Can you contact those searching?"

"Of course."

"Tell them to keep at it but to stay in groups and to be doubly alert. And have them look for a man named Balain."

"Balain? But—"

"That's a common name, Earl," interrupted Ursula. "It could belong to any of a hundred men even if it is genuine."

"He could be down there. Can't your scanners pick him out? Once we have him located we can go in after him." He saw the shake of her head. "No?"

"The scanners are all inoperative now. They must have blocked the terminals." She inhaled, breath hissing over her teeth. "Why are they doing this? Why?"

"Blocking the scanners?" Dumarest echoed his impatience. "Isn't that obvious? They don't want you to know what they're doing. My guess is that the leaders are arranging to escape under cover of a diversion. Had we waited for dawn they would have had plenty of time in which to vanish. As it is we could have them trapped." To the guard he said, "Make sure the area is surrounded and illuminated. If anyone tries to leave he is to be held for questioning. And tell the searchers to hurry."

As he turned away Ursula said, "I wasn't talking about the scanners, Earl. What I can't understand is why the Ohrm are rebelling against us? We've never done them any harm."

He said dryly, "Maybe they've grown tired of your telling them how to run their lives. It happens."

"Not here, Earl, it can't. It's—well, you don't understand."

"Try me."

"It's knowledge. They don't have it. They—" She broke off as a guard called from where he stood beside a light.

"They've found something! The explosives I think!"

The room was in a house set well within the complex; a bleak chamber, undecorated aside from crude patterns scrawled on the walls, illuminated by a single fluorescent tube. In the cold light Dumarest looked at a table, a bed, two chairs. The bed had been dragged from the corner to reveal a cavity gouged in the floor beneath. Boxes filled the opening.

"They're empty." A guard kicked at one with his boot. "All empty."

Dumarest kneeled and picked one up and turned it in his hands. It was small, the construction strong, the walls thick and padded with a synthetic quilting on the inside. He sniffed at it and ran a finger over the interior.

"Well?" Ursula was impatient. "Is that what we were looking for?"

"Yes, but we've arrived too late." Dumarest rose, dropping the box. "They've gone and taken the stuff with them."

"They could still be in the area."

"No. That guard we heard scream and the others who were killed must have run into the rebels making their escape. That's why they had to die. If the men had been in position a little earlier—" But it was useless to regret what could not be altered. "Who lives here?"

"Lived." The guard was precise. "Masak."

"Alone?" Dumarest studied the room with greater care. Even if not married he could have shared with a friend and certainly fellow conspirators would have spent time with him. The hollow holding the boxes proved that; one man would have needed help to gouge it out and dispose of the dirt. The boxes too would have required more than one to carry. "Are there other rooms attached?"

A kitchen and bathroom comprised the whole. A single person's accommodation as decided by the Choud. Dumarest had known worse.

"Find out who lives in the adjoining rooms," he said. "Get them. Don't frighten them but bring them here to me." As the guards left he moved to touch the walls. They echoed when he rapped them and he guessed they were of hollow brick coated with plaster. He said, "We have a chance, Ursula. These walls are thin and it's possible that others could have heard what was being said in here."

A small chance and one which dwindled as he questioned those brought to him. An old man who lived on the kitchen side and who was almost totally deaf. A woman who lived to the rear of the bedroom and who had a baby at her breast.

"Sometimes I'd hear things," she admitted. "Laughter and cheering and when I did I'd bang on the wall. Lately I've been busy with the child."

Too busy as was the young man who lived in the rooms against the bedroom.

"I'm out a lot," he said. "Working in the fields and when I get back home I'm too tired to do much more than sleep. I didn't hear anything and I don't know what went on."

"Failure, Earl," said Ursula as the man left. "There's no one else."

"One more," he corrected. "The rooms back of the bedroom aren't exactly in line. They're offset a little and the corner of one overlaps this chamber. We've still a chance."

One which faded as he saw the person who occupied the room. An old woman who blinked and cringed and backed as he stepped forward to take her arm.

"Relax, mother," he soothed. "No one is going to hurt you."

"Men," she said in a thin, dry voice. "Running and pushing people about and all that screaming. It wasn't like this in the old days. I lived in a bigger place then with Arold and my two sons. They've gone now and only I'm left." She sucked at her lips. "Should have left me," she said. "That was my house. They should have let me keep it."

"It was too large for you," said Ursula. "How could you have kept it clean?"

Logic which had no place in the old woman's world. She glared and turned away then halted as Dumarest stepped before her.

"They made a mistake, mother," he said. "You'll get your house back if you can help us. Now, let's play a little game. If this were your bedroom, where would your bed be positioned?" He nodded as she pointed. "The head against the wall, eh?"

"In the corner, mister. Where else?"

"And you need a lot of rest. At your age that's to be expected."

"I'm not too old to clean!"

"No, I'm sure you're not, but you like to go to bed early, right? And sleep."

"When I can," she grumbled. "When the noise lets me. All that scraping—why don't they do something about the rats?"

"Scraping," said Dumarest. "You heard a lot of scraping. When? Yesterday?"

"Days ago—I can't remember."

"And talking?"

"That too. Some people have no consideration for an old woman. If Arold and my sons were alive they'd have put a stop to it. Up half the night and sometimes until dawn. Talking and laughing and singing, too, at times. Young villains! Someone should do something about people like that."

"We're going to," promised Dumarest. "When we

find them. Now listen carefully, mother. Did you hear them a little while ago?"

"Yes. Bumping and banging and arguing. One of them had a loud voice and my head was against the wall."

"One of them? How many were there?"

"I don't know. Several, I think. One was called Balain. He was the one with the loud voice and he seemed to be giving the orders. Am I going to get my old house back? I can keep it clean."

"Yes," said Dumarest. "That's a promise." Gently he took the thin shoulders in his hands and looked into the faded eyes. "Now just one more thing, mother. Think carefully and tell me if Balain or any of the others said what they were going to do or where they were going."

"Into the city. They were going into the city."

"Among the Choud? And?"

"Get hurry."

"What?"

"Hurry," said the old woman impatiently. "The man with the loud voice said they had to get hurry. That's all I know. When do I get my house, Mister?"

Ursula said, after she had gone, "A waste of time, Earl. The old woman was almost senile. The men are probably far into the plains by now."

"What would they do with explosives in the plains? How would that destroy the Choud?"

"They can't destroy us, Earl."

A confidence he didn't share. Balain would have known what he was doing and speed would be important, but hurry? Get hurry? How could hurry be a target? Not hurry, then, but a word like it. One distorted by the wall and the onset of sleep. Urry? Huri?

Hury!

He said, "They're after Hury. Can they get it?"

"No." Ursula was positive. "It is guarded and there is only one way to reach it."

"Only one way? In a city? You really believe that?"

"Earl—"

"The sewers, Ursula! They're using the sewers!"

Chapter Thirteen

They ran beneath the jewel-like houses and the neatly kept terraces in a maze of twisting tunnels lit at intervals, damp, noisome, their brooding silence broken only by the susurration of water, the splash of adapted life.

"Rats." Ursula shivered as something darted into the water ahead to leave a trail of widening ripples. "This place must be alive with them."

"They won't hurt you."

"Maybe not." She didn't share Dumarest's confidence. "I hate the creatures. They could be everywhere."

If so they stayed out of sight as did other things which had made the subterranean complex their home. Webs festooned the glowing bowls of luminescence, their delicate, lace-like strands turning the cold glare into a nacreous glow which was reflected in broad lines of deposited slime on the curving sides of the passages and the raised concrete platform which provided dry footing. Bridges crossed the catwalk at intervals to provide access to branches and tributary passages. Echoes rose from the impact of their feet to die murmuring in the distance.

In the lead Dumarest halted, dropping to his knees as he examined the path. He rubbed at the surface, examined the grime on his finger, looked again before rising. Ursula looked at him.

"Earl?"

"We could have found their trail. One must have slipped and the edge of his shoe had scraped the concrete."

A guard said, "It could have happened weeks ago."

"No. The mark is recent or it would have been washed clean of fragments." Dumarest stared ahead to where the tunnel branched. "Send men ahead to search for further traces."

They edged past, the beams of their flashlights making hard circles of brilliance against the stained walls, the turgid water. Dumarest felt the woman close to his side. She was shivering beneath her cloak.

"You're cold," he said. "You should have waited on the surface."

"No." She stared at the bobbing lights. "Why don't they hurry?"

"Give them time." Dumarest saw a light steady and heard the call. "They've found something."

A patch of lichen had been scraped from a wall to leave a relatively light patch. Dumarest examined it, felt the ripped patch of primitive growth, and looked at the woman.

"Would this take them in the right direction?"

"They could have taken either path. The other would take them to a main junction and they would have to swing around the initial processing area. This would take them to the tributary inlets from the west."

"This is the way they came," said Dumarest. The marks could have been deliberately placed but the odds were against it. Amateur conspirators would have no time or thought for such deceptions and, as yet, they wouldn't know they were being followed. "Let everyone keep a watch for more signs and avoid making any noise."

The tunnels were sounding tubes and small sounds

would be magnified. Something which worked both ways but, though Dumarest had called a halt several times in order to listen, he'd heard nothing.

"Hurry," said Ursula. "We must hurry!"

A reversal of her previous confidence when she had been certain nothing could threaten the Choud. Only when she'd learned of an alternative route to Hury had she displayed a nervous anxiety. One shared by the guards.

Dumarest thinned his lips as one called to him from where he'd halted ahead.

"Keep your voice down, damn you! What is it?"

"A branch." The man pointed. "Which way do we go? Left or right?"

"Ursula?" Then, as she made no answer Dumarest snapped, "What's the matter? Doesn't any of you know how these sewers run?"

"Not the entire system."

"But you know where the target is?"

"Of course, but all these passages are confusing." She kept her voice low, words echoing to be lost in the susurration of the water. "A thing which will have to be rectified but who could have guessed we should need the information?"

"Those who built this place." Dumarest looked at the sides of the tunnel. "If they had had any sense they would have set up maps at strategic points.

"Earl, we have no time to look!"

"We'll look as we go on," he told her. "For now we'll split." His gestures divided the party. "You will take the right-hand tunnel while we take the left. If you hit another junction, split again if you have to. Keep searching until you find something. If you do, slow down and act with caution. We don't want to alert the men we're looking for. And remember—it won't help anyone if you get yourselves hurt."

They pressed on, the passages smaller now, the walls more thickly slimed. Beside the raised platform the water rushed past with increased velocity and the air was heavy with noxious odors. An open area gave some relief, the domed roof studded with lights, the walls pierced with rounded openings.

"A sector junction," said Ursula. "We go that way, I think."

Dumarest looked at the opening she had pointed out."

"Are you sure?"

"Yes, I—" She broke off, clutching his arm. "For God's sake what was that?"

A cry which echoed all around them, low, mournful, a wail which hung like a dirge. It came again, followed by a high-pitched ululation, a deep booming, a sound which resembled a snarl. Cries made by injured men, distorted, magnified, sent to stir the air in deceptive vibrations.

"Balain," said Dumarest. "The others must have found him."

And had been careless despite his warning. Dumarest looked down at a crumpled figure staring upward with sightless eyes. At another with a charred hole above his heart, a third with a crushed skull, a fourth and fifth burned and lying where they had fallen. Another lying with head and arms in the water as if to follow the one who had floated down to guide the living to the scene.

"Ambushed," said Dumarest. "The fools! I warned them to be careful."

"How?" The guard had been sick and stood beside his own vomit. "How did it happen?"

"They were careless. They talked or laughed or let their equipment strike against the wall. They were too confident and they paid for it." Dumarest stared down the passage, at the open mouth of a side tunnel, at a ledge which rested above eye level. "They were here, waiting, and found easy targets."

"The bastards!" The man wanted revenge. "Let's get them!"

Dumarest caught Ursula by the arm as she made to follow the others. They were acting without thought despite the grim evidence of what thoughtlessness could do. They would run and make noise and warn those ahead and again the tunnels would echo to the cries of dying men.

Things he explained as she fought to break his grip.

"Earl, you're letting them kill themselves!"

"I can't stop them." He was grimly practical. "But they will draw the enemy fire and pin them down. If they learn sense those left alive will know what to do after the initial contact. But there is no point in your taking a senseless risk."

"I'm not a coward!"

"And not a fool either, I hope." Dumarest released her arm, listening to the sudden outburst of noise, the cries which echoed down the tunnel. "That's it. Now let's see what we can do."

Another wide area lay beyond the end of the tunnel, a guard lying sprawled in the opening, blood thick around his throat, the feathers which tufted his flesh. The arrow had killed, ripping as it struck, the barbed head shredding delicate tissues. Another moaned as he sat with his back against a wall clutching his stomach. Blood pulsed between his fingers and the cloth of his uniform reeked with the stench of burned fabric.

Dumarest said, "What happened?"

"We found them. I heard a hiss and Riup dropped. Then there was a flash and I got burned." He sucked in his breath. "The beam hit me across the guts."

"Show me." Dumarest lifted the bloodied hands and examined the wound. The man had been lucky. "You'll live. Where are the others?"

"They went after the enemy. The firing came from up there." His head jerked toward the upper regions of the domed area. "There's a stair and the others went up it. I think one got hit."

More than one. Dumarest looked down at the sprawled bodies lying on the lower treads. One had fallen victim to an arrow. Higher up the flight a figure sprawled, head downward, one hand extended as if to clutch at the crossbow inches from his fingers.

"Kumate," said Ursula looking at his face. "The supervisor of the upper plantation. I always thought he was a happy man."

Dumarest made no comment. He stood, looking upward, the laser he carried poised in his hand. As the woman rose from her inspection he said, "Stay back and under cover."

"Why?" She lifted her own weapon. "I can use this as well as anyone."

"And die as bravely?"

"If I have to, yes."

He said bluntly, "I don't want you to die, Just stay out of the way until this is over. The guards may have been able to finish it but I doubt it. If any of the Ohrm are still alive they'll be waiting for us to pass through that door."

It gaped at the head of the stairs, a narrow portal, arched, glowing with a bluish light. Within it lay a dead man, another of the Ohrm, his body marked with many charred holes. Dumarest paused as he neared it, looking, straining his senses to catch any sound or flicker of light. He heard nothing but a faint humming and the light glowed with a steady luminosity.

Ursula said in a whisper, "They must have retreated, Earl. They ran before the guards. They couldn't have expected a second group to be following them."

"Two dead," he said as quietly. "There had to be more."

"They could be lying inside. It could be over."

"Then where are the guards?"

"They, too, perhaps—" She broke off and shook her head. "I don't know. Earl, tell me what to do. You're the expert."

"I told you."

"Not that!"

"Then be careful. Don't stand too close to me and keep to one side. Watch for movement. If you see any, fire without hesitation." He added, "I'm going inside. Count to three and follow."

He moved forward, running, jumping as a foot rested on a body to land to one side, to spring again as he scanned the chamber. A litter of bodies lay on the floor, some of them guards.

"Earl?" Ursula had followed. She fell silent at his gesture, followed the movement of his hand. A spiral staircase lay at one end of the room terminating in an opening above. As she watched it Dumarest checked the bodies.

The Ohrm were all dead aside from one who breathed with a liquid gurgling and blew bubbles of blood from his stained lips. None carried explosives. One of the dead guards had an arrow in his heart. Counting them, adding those lying below, Dumarest found one to be short. Upstairs?

He reached the foot and began to climb the spiral, laser held in readiness, attention concentrated on the opening above. Halfway up he caught a transient gleam as of a firefly burning in the night. Higher and he froze, listening, aware of the instinct which sent messages of warning; the signals he had long learned to trust.

Looking at the opening, trusting the woman was watching, he made gestures with his free hand.

"What—" With sudden understanding Ursula knew. Without a break she added, "—do you think, Earl? Did the guards get them all? That Ohrm over there, is it the one we're looking for? Here, let me help you turn him over."

She walked across the floor, emphasizing the sound of her footsteps, running to halt and gasp as if bending and lifting a heavy weight.

A deception which worked.

Dumarest saw the glint, the loom of mass and fired as a man thrust his head, shoulders and crossbow over the edge of the opening. As he fired again the constricting finger tightened in the death shock, and the vicious hum of the released string joined the savage hiss of the arrow as it passed close enough to catch Dumarest's hair.

Before it had fallen to the floor he was up and through the opening, leaping to one side to stand poised, eyes searching, seeing yet another stairway, the bulk of a machine, the sprawled figure of a guard.

"Earl!" Ursula appeared in the opening, tripping as her foot hit the dead man, stumbling to save herself from falling with a hand pressed against the enigmatic machine. "Did you get him? Balain, is he dead?"

A question answered as a man stepped from behind the shielding bulk of the machine to close his arm around her throat, the forearm pressed against her windpipe as the snort of the laser he held pressed hard against her temple.

"Drop your gun! Drop it!" As she obeyed he snapped, "You, too, Earl." Throw down that laser. Do it or I'll burn her brains out!"

"Of course, Balain." Dumarest threw aside the weapon. "Or should it be Eian?"

Calmly he looked at the handler of the *Sivas*.

The man was as he remembered, short, stocky, a little inclined to fat, attributes emphasized by the Ohrm clothing he wore. Held by the locking arm, Ursula said blankly, "Eian? The handler? Earl, he's dead!"

"No, he just wanted everyone to think that and it was easily arranged. A man murdered and dressed in his uniform to be rendered unrecognizable by the blast. Which is why you arranged it, Eian. A neat method of covering your tracks."

"You knew?"

"I guessed. Explosives such as carried by the *Sivas* can't be detonated with a laser even if the beam were powerful enough to burn through the packing. The weapons used by the guards aren't strong enough. So why did the explosives blow? They had to be fitted with detonators and no one in his right mind would have moved primed charges and risked an accidental explosion. So it shouldn't have been accidental." Dumarest added casually, "Do you intend throttling the woman? If not I'd suggest you ease the pressure of your arm."

"If you try anything—"

"Try what? You have the gun." Dumarest displayed his empty hands. "But the woman could do you an injury if she put her mind to it and, while you're busy killing her—" He smiled as the man cursed and pushed Ursula to one side. "That's better."

She said, rubbing her throat, "Why, Earl? Why?"

"For money." Dumarest kept his eyes on the handler. "For a lot of money."

"For a world!" The man sucked in his breath. "I had a plan. It would have worked like a clock but for an accident. It was perfect."

"But you misjudged the blast," said Dumarest. "You used too much explosive or triggered it to blow at the wrong second. The engine was hit and the *Sivas* was grounded."

"And you started to nose around. If it hadn't been for that none of this would have happened." The gesture of the laser took in the man lying dead at the opening, those lower down. "A couple of days and the ship would have left. There would have been all the time in the world to complete the plan. Instead you had to get suspicious. That business in the cold-store, Pellia thought you were giving the dead a blessing but I knew better."

"Which is why you gave orders to have me killed?"

"You were getting too close and I couldn't afford to take chances. There was too much at stake. Money—all the money you could ever hope to want. And more.

Power, the real kind, I'd have been a king. I can still be a king."

"Money," said Dumarest. "Let's stick to the money." He heard the woman suck in her breath but ignored her. "How? Where is it to come from?"

"Tekoa. The pods they suck—or haven't you learned about that yet? No, I suppose not, you've only been hours on this world and have kept yourself pretty damned busy. It's the main export. One pod if you're feeling low will set you up. Two will put you on a mountain. Three will lift you up to the stars. More than that—" He shrugged. "That's why Tuvey is so keen to keep this place a secret. He's got a monopoly."

"Which you wanted."

"Which I have." The laser lifted a little. "It came more messy than I'd intended but it's mine just the same."

"Balain," mused Dumarest. "The friend of the Ohrm. Teaching the oppressed the secrets of successful revolution. They overthrow their rulers and you ride along for fringe benefits. Let's hope they will last."

"Fringe benefits? Is that what you think?" Anger convulsed the rounded face. "I've go it all. Do you understand? It's all mine. The tekoa, this world, everything. If it hadn't been for you it would have been easy. I'd planned it down to the last detail. But a dancer's pimp had to get nosy. I ought to burn out your guts for interfering."

"I didn't."

"Would the Choud have searched the Ohrm houses but for you? Would they have dreamed of the possibility of a rebellion if you hadn't opened your mouth? I owe you a lot, you bastard!"

Dumarest said, "Why did you want the explosives?"

"Couldn't you figure that out?" Eian glanced at Ursula. "She knows. Haven't you told him about Hury yet? How you depend on it." To Dumarest he said, "Do you take me for a fool? How the hell did you think I was going to win this world? Trust a bunch of ignorant yokels to be grateful? That would have been stupid. No, I was going to blackmail the Choud. I'm still going to blackmail them. In a day they'll be eating out of my hand."

"And calling you their king?"

"If I wanted, yes."

Ursula said urgently, "Please, where are the explosives? I'll promise all the pods you need, money, too, and, of course, safe conduct if you will tell me."

"You're too late," said the handler. "They're stacked and I don't have to tell you where. But I'll tell you what will happen if you don't do as I say. You see this?" His free hand lifted a small, black box from a pocket. See the two buttons? This is a radio remote control. If I press the red button the explosives will blow in twenty seconds. Unless I press the green one within fifteen nothing can stop the blast. Neat, eh? I figure it'll—" He yelled as Ursula dived toward him. "You fool! Get back! Back!"

He fired as Dumarest dropped his hand to his knife, fired again as the steel rose to hurtle toward him, the blade turning red hot as the beam hit it, searing metal striking his face to hit the bone above the eye, to glance downward to plunge into the orb, blood and lymphatic fluids hissing and creating wisps of steam as it came to rest in the brain beneath.

"Ursula?"

"He missed!" She slapped at the flames marring the cerulean beauty of her hair. "Well, almost. Where is the box."

Dumarest reached for it as he dragged free his knife. Eian still clutched it and, dying, he had done his worst. The red button was depressed.

"God!" She turned and raced for the stairs. "Dear God give me time!"

"Come back!" Seconds had already passed and more were flying as she climbed the treads. "Eian could have been bluffing."

And, if not, she could be running to her death.

He called to the wind. Ignoring him she raced on, reaching the top of the stairs as he set foot on the bottom, out of sight by the time he dived through the upper opening, only the rap of her running feet echoing through the upper chamber.

One which held more enigmatic bulks and had a roof supported on massive struts. Instruments glowed from humped machines and the air was filled with the taint of ozone and coolants.

"Ursula?" Dumarest ran forward, no longer hearing the patter of her feet. "Ursula!"

A metallic tinkle and he turned to run down a narrow passage. Another and he saw her busy at heaped packages wired into a compact whole, a rounded box set among them, a ruby light glowing on its surface.

"Ursula! Get—"

The world exploded into livid flame.

Chapter Fourteen

He had died and was drifting in the void and his decaying brain was projecting the stored images in a series of scintillant flashes. The massed explosives, Ursula turning, the ruby light, the sudden gush of flame which turned her blue into scarlet; clothing, hair, skin all vanishing as the shock wave of the blast had reached toward him faster than he could think.

But now that he was dead and drifting there was time for thought. Ursula was dead and she had been of the Choud.

Eian, dying, had taken his revenge and destroyed the Hury.

The Choud. The Hury.

The *Choudhury*!

The obvious which had nagged at his subconcious and which he had failed to recognize until it was too late. Instead he had formed a wrong conclusion—a mistake which had cost him the chance of finding the whereabouts of Earth.

"Earl!" Someone was calling him, but who would waste time calling the dead?

"Earl, wake up. Wake up, Earl. Please wake up!"

A noise which gave him no peace. One which sent the darkness rolling back to leave a thin, pale, illumination pressing like a ghost light against his eyes. Fingers caught the hand he lifted to his face.

"No. It's all right. You were burned and had to be bandaged. Tuvey—"

"My eyes?"

"Should be healed now. Please, Earl, let me do it."

He lowered his hand and felt the touch of chill metal; scissors which snipped the bandages from the upper part of his face. As they fell away he blinked at the figure which stood beside the bed.

Kalin?

She looked the same but was misted against the light which caught her hair and turned it into flame. But the color was wrong, and as she turned, the flame changed to gold as the face became familiar.

"Pellia?"

"You recognize me. Good." She leaned closer, her fingers cool as they touched his face, the region around the eyes. "You were lucky, Earl. Instinct saved your eyes. You threw up an arm to shield them and the blast flung you back behind some cover." She added quietly, "The woman—"

"Is dead. I know." Dumarest sat upright on the bed and fought a momentary nausea. "How long?"

"Two days. We found you, and the captain told us what to do. Sardia helped."

With slow-time which had accelerated his metabolism so as to stretch hours into days. With intravenous feeding and selected hormones to mend the broken ribs and aid the replacement of destroyed tissue.

"It was completely destroyed, Earl." Pellia rubbed her hands over the bedcover like a small girl who is reluctant to break bad news. "Balain carried out his threat. He was a great man."

"He was a self-seeking animal and you're better off without him." Dumarest threw his legs over the side of the bed. He was naked. "Where are my clothes?"

They were burnt, seared, protective mesh bared to the light. Only the boots and belt remained relatively untouched. The knife would have to be honed and retempered as the garments needed to be refurbished but they were things easily managed.

As he stepped from the room with its bed and medical apparatus, Tuvey came into view down the corridor. Etallia was with him carrying a large jug. As they met, the captain halted her, took the jug from her hands and handed it to Dumarest.

"Here, I guess you could use this." It was basic. As Dumarest swallowed the energizing liquid Tuvey continued, "It's a hell of a mess. The only good thing about it is that Shartan was wrong about the generator. It doesn't need a replacement. We'll be ready to leave in a few hours."

"I want passage."

"Yes, I thought you might, and I guess you've earned it. Eian—" Tuvey broke off and looked at his clenched hands. "That bastard must have been crazy. He rode with me for years and all the time he was planning to ruin a world. He did ruin it. Ath will never be the same again.

"It could be better."

"Maybe." Tuvey sounded doubtful. "But it won't be the same. Finished with that jug?" He took it and handed it to the woman. "I owe her something," he explained. "She was good to me in the past and I'm trying to make things a little easy for her."

"Aren't the Ohrm helping?"

"Of course," said Pellia. "We are doing everything we can."

Which needn't be enough. Dumarest said, "They need you, Captain. The Choud and the Ohrm both. You can help them. They need books and educational apparatus; hypnotic tutors and the like. You can bring them in together with agricultural machinery; nothing too elaborate but something to relieve them of endless labor. In a few years, with your aid, Ath will have gained new life and have a viable culture. Give passage to a few monks—they'll be glad to help."

And would be grateful for the opportunity. The Church of Universal Brotherhood could use a relatively untouched world and would be kind to the innocence now prevailing. Tuvey thought about it, weighing the advantages, nodding as he reached a decision.

"Hell, why not? I'm not going to live forever and I'll still hold the monopoly. If they can increase tekoa production I'll double trips and profit. And it could be fun to take a hand in the shaping of things. I might even retire and take up land to the south." Reaching out he took Etallia by the arm. "We leave at sunset."

Outside the hospital the city looked as he remembered and then little things gained his attention: men and women, gaily dressed who wandered without apparent purpose. The swimmers sitting beside the water who looked as if they had sat there for days and would continue to sit unless someone led them away. Others, the Ohrm, who walked with a new assurance and looked at the jewel-like houses with possessive eyes.

At his side Pellia said, "Earl, we need you. Please don't leave us. You could be our new leader. Now that Balain is dead we haven't anyone to follow. We don't know what to do." She ended plaintively, "I never guessed it would be like this."

A sudden change which hurt as all changes do. An alteration in the previously smooth-running scheme of things and the unaccustomed burden of responsibility. How many of them had thought beyond the glittering lies the handler had fed them? How many had been capable?

He said, "Pellia, when a woman gives birth it hurts, right?"

"Yes, Earl, but not for long."

"And this won't hurt for long either." She hadn't

grasped the analogy. "A revolution is like a birth," Dumarest explained patiently. "Something new is created and creation is always accompanied with pain. At the moment you feel lost. The Choud are no longer telling you what to do and when to do it and how it should be done. Now you are having to think for yourselves. You are having to make decisions." Then, as she continued to stare at him, he snapped, Damn it, girl, did you imagine it would be easy?"

"Balain—"

"Wanted to be a dictator. He wanted to take over from the Choud and to become a despot. Thank your gods he didn't succeed. If he had you'd have learned what it was to be a slave. Now you've got to learn to stand up and act and think for yourselves."

"Earl why don't you stay and teach us?"

"I can't."

"You could have a house, the best there is, and we would do just what you told us to do. You could have anything you wanted. Anything. Earl, please!"

A world which he could use as a plaything, one he could guide as he wished. The tekoa would provide a fortune, the Ohrm willing servants, the Choud—he didn't want to think about the Choud. About what had been done to them.

"Earl?"

"No." He looked at the sky. The sun was past zenith and time was running out. "Where can I find Sardia?"

"I don't know." Woman-like she was sullen at his refusal. "At Cornelius's house, I guess."

She came to meet him as he turned from the path, crossing the lawn to stand before him and search his face with her eyes. Her own held shadows and a peculiar hurt and age rested more heavily on her face than he remembered.

"Earl!" Her hand lifted to touch his cheek. "I was so worried!"

"There was no need."

"You didn't see what you looked like after you'd been dragged from beneath the wreckage. And there was no one at the hospital who could help. If—"

"I know," he said. "Pellia told me."

"She learned," said Sardia. "And will learn more. They will all learn." Bitterly she added, "So much for victory."

"It was an accident. They didn't know."

"They didn't care!"

He repeated flatly, "They didn't know. Did you? Did I? We should have guessed but we didn't and we had all the clues. The way the Choud would tilt back the head and seem to listen and blink after the connection was broken. The things they knew without being told—of me leaving you after the dance, the subjects discussed, the whereabouts of others and the things they had done. The knowledge they had."

The hobbies taken up and dropped to make way for another. The gracious living. The certainty of supremacy. The ship they had arrived in.

The *Choudhury*.

The name they had taken. The name they had given to the computer to which they had all been linked.

He remembered the rounded nodule he had felt beneath the woman's scalp, the lack of anything similar on the heads of the Ohrm. Divergent stock could have accounted for the differentiation but he had been told they were both of common origin. And Ursula had known about Earth.

Not Ursula—Hury.

"Earl?" Sardia was looking at him, her eyes anxious. "Is something wrong?"

Dumarest looked down at his hands and forced himself to relax the clenched fingers. Forced himself, too, to fight the sick regret tearing at his insides, the anger at his own stupidity. Why hadn't he recognized the obvious sooner? Ursula could have told him about Earth—*but so could any other of the Choud*!

The information had been stored in the computer taken from the old vessel; one used as a general-purpose library to deliver information to all fitted with the engrafted transceivers. The strength of the Choud and their ultimate weakness.

He said, "Where is Cornelius?"

He sat before the easel in the studio with the high, arched windows which framed the vista beyond. Paint was thick on his fingers, eyes fastened to the work as, tongue thrust between his teeth, he painstakingly daubed splotches on the ruined canvas.

"It's gone," said Sardia bitterly. "All gone. He doesn't know anything. He can talk and walk and that's about all. All the rest has been forgotten."

Not forgotten—never learned.

Dumarest looked at the man, wondering what it must have been like to have the answer to any question immediately at hand. There had been no need to memorize a single fact; a thought and it was delivered. As had been the data needed to take up pottery, weaving, painting, architecture, medicine, dancing—all that had been painfully learned over the millennia, condensed, refined, at hand at any moment. The accumulated knowledge which had made the Choud the masters of their world.

Cornelius turned and saw them and smiled. "Look," he said. "Look."

"That's good." Sardia's voice held tears. "Very good. But try and get the lines into a pattern which can be recognized. Two lines set opposite to each other and joined by a curve at the top. See?" Her hand lifted to point at the window. "Just like that. Now draw me a picture I can recognize as a window."

"A window?"

"An opening set into a wall to admit light," said Dumarest. The man was like a child. "You must know what a window is."

"An opening," said Cornelius. "One set in a wall to admit light."

A child, but like a child he would learn as all the Choud would learn. As they had to learn if they were to survive.

"A moon," said Dumarest. "Think of a moon. Describe it to me. Tell me where it can be found?" He looked at the blank face and uncomprehending eyes. "Terra," he said. "The moon as seen from Earth. Where is Earth?"

A hope which died as Cornelius frowned and turned back to his painting. Once he could have answered with facts and figures, given the spatial coordinates and so pinpointed the location of the world which had become a legend. A simple question would have done it—why hadn't he asked it?

So close!

So very close!

"Earl! You're looking as you did in the garden! As if you wanted to kill someone. But Cornelius isn't to blame. You can't—"

"No." Dumarest shook his head. "No, he isn't to blame and I won't hurt him. Have you assembled his paintings? Are they here?" He walked across the room to where canvases lay piled on a table. "Tuvey is leaving at sunset."

"I know. I'm not leaving with him." Sardia came to stand at his side, to look as he was looking at the topmost portrait. It was of the degraded angel. "You spot the resemblance?"

"This isn't you."

"No? How can you be so sure, Earl? What do you know of me? Cornelius saw beneath the skin and into the heart." She reached out to touch it. "It's yours if you want it."

He lifted it without answering and looked at the one below.

"The suspended man," she explained, "He told me about it. He had yet to finish it. The face—" She drew in her breath.

"His face."

"Once, yes, but he must have added touches since I saw it last. Now it resembles someone else." She looked at him. "He must have done it after you'd met at the dinner. After I'd made a fool of myself."

"After you'd danced," he corrected. "If there is a fool on this world it isn't you. So you're staying?"

"Yes. They need help and I can give it. And I'm hoping that he'll get it back." She glanced at Cornelius. "It still has to be there. Genius isn't something you learn from a book or gain from a computer. He has it and maybe I can get it to flower again. It may take years, even a lifetime, but it's something I have to do. Can you understand that?"

"Yes," said Dumarest. "I can understand."

"We have an agreement, remember?"

"Forget it."

"I can't do that. These paintings are of value and should compensate you. You could take them to a man I know and let him sell them for you on a commission basis." She saw his expression. "No?"

"No." He added, "Cornelius could need them. They might trigger his latent talent or something."

"Then take one at least," she urged. "This one. I'd like you to have it. To give you something by which to remember me."

"I don't need that to remember you, Sardia." Dumarest made no move to take the painting. "And I need to travel light."

With his clothes and knife and little else aside from his memories but they would burden enough. As would be the pain he had known, the broken hopes, the aching loneliness.

She turned, looking at Cornelius, seeing him staring at her, one hand extended. He smiled as she took it in her own, comforted, satisfied and contented as a man could be who has found the thing necessary to his happiness. The thing most men needed; a woman who loved him and whom he could love. A simple thing but Dumarest—Dumarest needed to find a world.

Recommended for Star Warriors!

The Dorsai Novels of Gordon R. Dickson

- ☐ DORSAI! (#UE1342—$1.75)
- ☐ SOLDIER, ASK NOT (#UE1339—$1.75)
- ☐ TACTICS OF MISTAKE (#UW1279—$1.50)
- ☐ NECROMANCER (#UE1353—$1.75)

The Commodore Grimes Novels of A. Bertram Chandler

- ☐ THE BIG BLACK MARK (#UW1355—$1.50)
- ☐ THE WAY BACK (#UW1352—$1.50)
- ☐ STAR COURIER (#UY1292—$1.25)

The Dumarest of Terra Novels of E. C. Tubb

- ☐ JACK OF SWORDS (#UY1239—$1.25)
- ☐ SPECTRUM OF A FORGOTTEN SUN (#UY1265—$1.25)
- ☐ HAVEN OF DARKNESS (#UY1299—$1.25)
- ☐ PRISON OF NIGHT (#UW1364—$1.50)

The Daedalus Novels of Brian M. Stableford

- ☐ THE FLORIANS (#UY1255—$1.25)
- ☐ CRITICAL THRESHOLD (#UY1282—$1.25)
- ☐ WILDEBLOOD'S EMPIRE (#UW1331—$1.50)

To order these titles,
see coupon on the
last page of this book.

GREAT NOVELS OF HEROIC ADVENTURES ON EXOTIC WORLDS

- [ ] LAMARCHOS by Jo Clayton. (#UW1354—$1.50)
- [ ] DINOSAUR BEACH by Keith Laumer. (#UW1332—$1.50)
- [ ] THE GODS OF XUMA by David J. Lake. (#UW1360—$1.50)
- [ ] THE BIG BLACK MARK by A. Bertram Chandler. (#UW1355—$1.50)
- [ ] THE WAY BACK by A. Bertram Chandler. (#UW1352—$1.50)
- [ ] THE GRAND WHEEL by Barrington J. Bayley. (#UW1318—$1.50)
- [ ] THE OVERLORDS OF WAR by Gerard Klein. (#UW1313—$1.50)
- [ ] BENEATH THE SHATTERED MOONS by Michael Bishop. (#UW1305—$1.50)
- [ ] EARTHCHILD by Doris Piserchia. (#UW1308—$1.50)
- [ ] ARMADA OF ANTARES by Alan Burt Akers. (#UY1227—$1.25)
- [ ] RENEGADE OF KREGEN by Alan Burt Akers. (#UY1271—$1.25)
- [ ] KROZAIR OF KREGEN by Alan Burt Akers. (#UW1288—$1.50)
- [ ] ALDAIR IN ALBION by Neal Barrett, Jr. (#UY1235—$1.25)
- [ ] ALDAIR, MASTER OF SHIPS by Neal Barrett, Jr. (#UW1326—$1.50)
- [ ] WARLORD OF GHANDOR by Del DowDell. (#UW1315—$1.50)
- [ ] THE RIGHT HAND OF DEXTRA by David J. Lake. (#UW1290—$1.50)
- [ ] THE WILDINGS OF WESTRON by David J. Lake. (#UW1306—$1.50)
- [ ] KIOGA OF THE WILDERNESS by William L. Chester. (#UW1253—$1.50)
- [ ] ONE AGAINST A WILDERNESS by William L. Chester. (#UW1280—$1.50)
- [ ] KIOGA OF THE UNKNOWN LAND by William L. Chester. (#UJ1378—$1.95)
- [ ] INTERSTELLAR EMPIRE by John Brunner. (#UE1362—$1.75)

To order these titles,
see coupon on the
last page of this book.

- [ ] **THE 1978 ANNUAL WORLD'S BEST SF.** Leading off with Varley, Haldeman, Bryant, Ellison, Bishop, etc.
(#UJ1376—$1.95)

- [ ] **THE 1977 ANNUAL WORLD'S BEST SF.** Featuring Asimov, Tiptree, Aldiss, Coney, and a galaxy of great ones. An SFBC Selection. (#UE1297—$1.75)

- [ ] **THE 1976 ANNUAL WORLD'S BEST SF.** A winner with Fritz Leiber, Brunner, Cowper, Vinge, and more. An SFBC Selection. (#UW1232—$1.50)

- [ ] **THE 1975 ANNUAL WORLD'S BEST SF.** The authentic "World's Best" featuring Bester, Dickson, Martin, Asimov, etc. (#UW1170—$1.50)

- [ ] **THE DAW SCIENCE FICTION READER.** The unique anthology with a full novel by Andre Norton and tales by Akers, Dickson, Bradley, Stableford, and Tanith Lee.
(#UW1242—$1.50)

- [ ] **THE BEST FROM THE REST OF THE WORLD.** Great stories by the master of sf writers of Western Europe.
(#UE1343—$1.75)

- [ ] **THE YEAR'S BEST FANTASY STORIES: 3.** Edited by Lin Carter, the 1977 volume includes C. J. Cherryh, Karl Edward Wagner, G.R.R. Martin, etc. (#UW1338—$1.50)

To order these titles, see coupon on the last page of this book.

Presenting MICHAEL MOORCOCK in DAW editions

The Elric Novels

- [ ] ELRIC OF MELNIBONE (#UW1356—$1.50)
- [ ] THE SAILOR ON THE SEAS OF FATE (#UY1270—$1.25)
- [ ] THE WEIRD OF THE WHITE WOLF (#UW1390—$1.50)
- [ ] THE VANISHING TOWER (#UW1406—$1.50)
- [ ] THE BANE OF THE BLACK SWORD (#UW1421—$1.50)
- [ ] STORMBRINGER (#UW1335—$1.50)

The Runestaff Novels

- [ ] THE JEWEL IN THE SKULL (#UW1419—$1.50)
- [ ] THE MAD GOD'S AMULET (#UW1391—$1.50)
- [ ] THE SWORD OF THE DAWN (#UW1392—$1.50)
- [ ] THE RUNESTAFF (#UW1422—$1.50)

The Oswald Bastable Novels

- [ ] THE WARLORD OF THE AIR (#UW1380—$1.50)
- [ ] THE LAND LEVIATHAN (#UY1214—$1.25)

Other Titles

- [ ] LEGENDS FROM THE END OF TIME (#UY1281—$1.25)
- [ ] A MESSIAH AT THE END OF TIME (#UW1358—$1.50)
- [ ] DYING FOR TOMORROW (#UW1366—$1.50)

DAW BOOKS are represented by the publishers of Signet and Mentor Books, THE NEW AMERICAN LIBRARY, INC.

THE NEW AMERICAN LIBRARY, INC.,
P.O. Box 999, Bergenfield, New Jersey 07621

Please send me the DAW BOOKS I have checked above. I am enclosing $_____ (check or money order—no currency or C.O.D.'s). Please include the list price plus 35¢ per copy to cover mailing costs.

Name_____

Address_____

City_____ State_____ Zip Code_____

Please allow at least 4 weeks for delivery